T0192958

Praise for

All Creatures Weird and Dangerous

Real and mythological animals play a huge role in our folklore and in our memory as a species. Things we cannot explain or are afraid of remain a giant part of our shared psychology. Dr. Timm Otterson provides a nice blend of traditional creatures of timeless legend and the modern science of veterinary medicine with a very readable recipe. Wanting to believe is what has kept Santa Claus, the Easter Bunny, and the shadowy animals of these fables alive. Sit back and enjoy these stories and meet a new legendary being with each chapter.
—**Kevin Fitzgerald**, DVM, *Animal Planet's "Emergency Vets"*

Ever wondered what your friendly neighborhood veterinarian gets up to when he or she is not busy vaccinating Fluffy or pulling thorns from Fido's paws? Well, if Timm Otterson's account of his dealings with "creatures weird and dangerous" is any indication, it may be a lot more interesting than you suspect. From the moment a local girl with a strange injured animal—it turns out to be a real-life specimen of the legendary Chupacabra—seeks his help while he's visiting Puerto Rico, Otterson's rapidly-evolving relationship with the brave new world of cryptozoology takes him (and his readers) on a roller coaster ride through a series of increasingly bizarre and entertaining incidents involving animal patients that are, well … let's just say highly unusual. Along the way, with an exquisite attention to routine details that makes his extraordinary experiences come alive for the reader, Otterson manages to educate us on the makings of a career in veterinary medicine, give us the flavor of a number of exotic, mostly wild places, introduce us to some pretty eccentric people, and even offer commentary on the ongoing global environmental crisis and our often feeble efforts to preserve endangered species.

At a time when social media spouts equal parts real scientific breakthrough and pseudo- or even phoney "science," the average layperson is often left to his or her own devices trying to determine which is which. Otterson's vision is of a world damaged and threatened by man's callousness toward nature, but where Mother Nature still has a few discoveries to be made, a few secrets to tell, a few tricks up her sleeve. Most of us expect to live out our lives without encountering a creature long thought to be extinct, or merely the stuff of legend—let alone being made responsible for its health and well-being. Otterson, the ever-helpful friend of creatures both mundane and fantastic, leaves the impression he didn't think his interest in nature would take him on an improbable journey through the world of strange and mysterious creatures either—until it did. Luckily, he's willing to take us along, and if you're like me, you will turn each page in eager anticipation of what new adventure—and what strange and possibly dangerous creature—lurks just ahead!

—**Paul Dyster,** former mayor of Niagara Falls, New York and life-long Great Lakes environmentalist

It is a basic truism that the American public believes that physicians and dentists treat all of our physical ailments and that the rest of the sufferings of the animal kingdom are the responsibilities of veterinarians. Every young veterinarian discovers this shortly after graduation when a mother brings in her son's sick hamster or a kind-hearted motorist finds an injured owl beside the road or a client pulls his or her ailing pet snake out of a cardboard box.

While most veterinarians end up specializing in farm animals or household pets, there are a very few that accept the challenge that if it is sick and walks, crawls, swims, or flies, they will undertake to relieve their suffering. And, for those that do, the world can be a very exciting place. Fortunately for us, Dr. Timm Otterson is one of those veterinarians, and he has written a wonderfully entertaining book detailing his adventures.

This is marvelous nonfiction and if you enjoy animals and exploration, you will love this book, and if you are a venturesome young person, you might even be inspired to become an animal doctor.

—**Michael Groves,** DVM, PhD, Dean Emeritus, LSU School of Veterinary Medicine

Such a treat to be taken on so many wonderful adventures and encounters. With each story, we become more engrossed and entranced. I found myself eagerly awaiting each chapter and smiling from ear to ear. Just delightful! Timm gives us permission to leave our own self contained world and, for a brief time, take a glimpse of a set of new possibilities. BRAVA!

—**Susan E. Wylegala**, DVM, former President of the New York State Veterinary Medical Society

Timm Otterson has a flair for storytelling combined with an economical writing style that effortlessly propels his subject matter forward. In *All Creatures Weird and Dangerous*, Dr. Otterson, writing through a veterinarian's lens, tells of chupacabras ... and other fantastic creatures in a fast-paced story that's sure to enchant readers.

—**Mark Sommer**, author of *Rocky Colavito: Cleveland's Iconic Slugger*

ALL CREATURES WEIRD
AND DANGEROUS

GUERNICA WORLD EDITIONS 45

ALL CREATURES WEIRD AND DANGEROUS

Timm Otterson, DVM

GUERNICA
World
EDITIONS

TORONTO—CHICAGO—BUFFALO—LANCASTER (U.K.)
2022

Michael Mirolla, general editor
Gary Clairman, editor
Interior design: Jill Ronsley, suneditwrite.com
Cover design: Allen Jomoc Jr.

Guernica Editions Inc.
287 Templemead Drive, Hamilton (ON), Canada L8W 2W4
2250 Military Road, Tonawanda, N.Y. 14150-6000 U.S.A.
www.guernicaeditions.com

Distributors:
Independent Publishers Group (IPG)
600 North Pulaski Road, Chicago IL 60624
University of Toronto Press Distribution (UTP)
5201 Dufferin Street, Toronto (ON), Canada M3H 5T8
Gazelle Book Services, White Cross Mills
High Town, Lancaster LA1 4XS U.K.

First edition.

Legal Deposit—First Quarter
Library of Congress Catalog Card Number: 2021947559
Library and Archives Canada Cataloguing in Publication
Title: All creatures weird and dangerous / Timm Otterson.
Names: Otterson, Timm, 1967- author.
Series: Guernica world editions ; 45.
Description: Series statement: Guernica world editions ; 45.
Identifiers: Canadiana (print) 20210333839 | Canadiana (ebook)
20210333847 | ISBN 9781771837088 (softcover) | ISBN 9781771837095 (EPUB)
Classification: LCC PS3615.T888 A64 2022 | DDC 813/.6—dc23

To Laurie, Nels, and Warren
—my wife, my son, and my father—
for your sense of adventure, curiosity, and appreciation
of the value of mischief.

CHAPTER ONE

Y ou would have to be deranged to expect to spend your vacation like this. In fact, the whole scene was absurd. We had traveled to Puerto Rico on a trip with my son's fourth grade class. He had been studying Spanish as part of an immersion program in the Buffalo Public Schools and we (my wife, son, and I) were a few days into our long-awaited trip to the Isla de Encantas with about ten students from his class, a number of their parents, and our favorite teacher, Señora Ramos. More importantly, for the moment, here I was, standing with my friend and fellow parent, Alvin, along with a Puerto Rican girl, staring at a strange and unconscious creature.

Why me, you ask? I'm a veterinarian. It's not unusual for veterinarians to be brought lost or injured creatures. Just the week before, a group of high school students were walking in front of our clinic on a lovely spring day in Buffalo, New York and found a small bird hopping around on the ground. A really small bird. A fledgling. The avian equivalent of a toddler. Mother Nature had decided it was time for him to leave the nest and kind of make it on his own. (The parents of most avian species typically help out the fledglings for a while.) The tiny bird was out on the grass looking pathetic so the kids wisely brought him into our clinic, which happened to be right near their school. I'm going to presume that you have seen a Black-capped Chickadee before. They are those cute tiny birds with black caps on their heads that will land on you when you are walking in the woods in places where people put out seed. This little guy was adorable. He was also apparently healthy per my exam so I advised the kids to return the bird to where they found him and let his parents look after his transition to avian independence.

Now the creature Alvin and I were staring at on this patio in Puerto Rico was not adorable. In fact, he was really horrific looking. I work in an all-feline clinic and have for a few decades now so my day-to-day practice has been just cats. Cats will keep you on your toes. The bite from a housecat has put a lot of my colleagues in the hospital. They may not be big, but they are strong and flexible and know how to use their teeth and eighteen claws. One cat bite can send you straight to the doctor and on to lots of penicillin.

Looking at this creature on the patio, I could not imagine what one bite could do. Alvin was about to have a nervous breakdown, and I could not blame him. The girl who brought the creature to us, however, was strangely calm. My Spanish language skills were rusty, and her English skills were no better. I'd grown up in Texas and had studied Spanish in school, but that was a long time ago. I was able to piece together that she had found this creature in her front yard lying beneath a plate glass door. It was late—after 10 pm. Alvin and I had spent the last couple nights staying up late drinking beer and our reasonable imitation of mojitos. We loved Puerto Rico and especially the evenings. These little native tree frogs called *coquís* would sing for hours. They actually would say "coquí" over and over again.

I had to give the girl credit for her resourcefulness. She had met my son earlier in the day as part of the cultural exchange. For the introduction, the kids had gone around in a circle and said something about their families. My son shared that his dad was a vet. A lot of ten-year-old kids want to be vets so he thought that would interest his new friends—and apparently he was right.

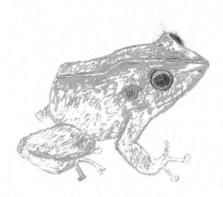

Common coqui
Eleutherodactylus coqui

So, long story short, this brave little girl found an injured creature late at night and brought it to the only hotel in this fishing village where the visiting veterinarian and his friend were having a nightcap or two. In retrospect, I am glad she did not bring her siblings and parents along, because I hate a scene—and man would this thing cause a scene. First of all, the creature was silvery and scaly: tight scales like snakes have. I would guess that it weighed about twenty pounds, and it was all muscle. It was about two feet long with a tapering tail that had almost a little fan at the tip. It had four short stocky legs all with talons, like a bird of prey. The head was cat-like with the big forward-facing eyes of a predator. The top of its head had a spiky comb like a satanic rooster, but its most striking feature was its mouth. It makes the hair on my neck stand up to think of those pointy teeth, almost a cross between a bat and a shark. This thing was definitely not an herbivore, but what was it? Then I noticed the wings—slight, long, bat-like wings that sort of tucked in behind his forelimbs. I kept looking it over and over and thinking, "What the hell is this?" When I came out of my focused state, I heard my friend muttering, "What the hell is this?" I'm pretty sure the little girl was muttering something similar in Spanish.

I snapped out of my reverie and returned to veterinary mode. I started asking myself the standard questions I would ask in daily practice. What are the clinical signs? Are there obvious injuries? Did this problem come on suddenly or is it chronic? And, most important: What can I do to help? For the most part, medicine in all species is the same. Whether it's a human or a cat or a fish, we all generally get the same problems. Viruses, bacteria, nutritional deficiencies, endocrine disorders, trauma—they affect us all. Given that our patients cannot talk with us, private practice veterinary medicine is a lot like being a pediatrician, but the problem before me now was more like being a wildlife, or maybe a zoo, vet. No one was going to help me figure this out. I would have to rely on my training and some common sense.

When faced with an exotic animal case, my zoo medicine colleagues have some real challenges and they are mostly the obvious ones you can likely think of yourself—fangs, horns, teeth, antlers, trunks, hooves, and poison, among other things. But likely the most dangerous quality of a wild animal is fear. A frightened animal is the most likely to hurt someone including itself. But fortunately, we veterinarians can use some rational thinking and the wealth of knowledge our profession has already learned from domestic animals. When presented with a sick hyena, my friend Dr. Victor at the Buffalo Zoo does his best to treat it like he would the dog he saw when in general practice. When there are problems with the giraffes, you treat them like cows with really long legs and necks. You treat the injured toucan in much the same way you treat the pet macaw. Sometimes you may have to improvise. This creature before us, however, was unlike any class of beast I had ever even dreamed of. My biggest fear with this creature was that it was going to wake up and maul us all. Fortunately, Alvin was getting his composure back and looking eager to help.

I started poking around and examining. I'm a creature of habit so I started in just like I would with the thousands of house cats I've seen. Eyes were intact. The irises were a glistening gold color with oval shaped pupils. The pupils were a little more dilated than I would expect for a normal whatever this was, although being unconscious likely distorted their state. The oral cavity was spectacular! So many teeth in almost overlapping rows. All the teeth were pyramid shaped and sharp. The long and slender tongue reminded me of a snake. The ears were small and pointed, and faced forward like you would expect in a predator, but they were not large like a bat so I doubt they were used for echolocation. When I looked at the odd pointed "comb" that ran longitudinally across the top of its head, a light bulb went off. This is a *Chupacabra*! As I looked at his face and skull, it all came back to me. I was holding the legendary creature of the Caribbean and South America. The face looked a lot like one of the sketches I had seen on websites.

I have always been interested in cryptozoology, "the study of mystical or hidden creatures," so, sometime in the past I must have wandered across the chupacabra online. In the mid-1990s, a series of unexplained injuries to livestock on Puerto Rico started a panic about a strange and dangerous creature haunting the island. The unfortunate name, which literally translates as "goat sucker," was given by a local comedian. Reports on the chupacabra's appearance vary greatly. I've seen sketches of them that range from the Creature from the Black Lagoon down to what appears to be a Chihuahua dog with mange and dental disease. The creature before me resembled the *Peuchen* described in Chilean folklore: long and snake-like with wings. The more I looked, the more impressed I was. His wings were amazing—delicate bones like a bat with a thin skin forming the wing. No fractures here. His torso looked fine. No scratches or broken ribs. His four muscular legs ended in digits that had the sharpness and strength of a falcon, and a pair of rear facing toes like a woodpecker, possibly designed for holding on to trees or a rock face.

As I looked at him, I could imagine this graceful creature soaring around on the seashore and then swooping up and easily hanging from rocks on a cliff edge. He would then drop down on some unsuspecting prey and devour it with these wonderful, horrible teeth. As we stared at his gray and silver scales, it dawned on me how hard it was to clearly see the creature. It was almost the perfect camouflage. If this guy was hanging in a tree above my head, I doubt that I would recognize him. People often mock cryptozoologists by saying that with all the people in the world wouldn't we commonly see a creature like this? Looking at him now, I can see how he could disappear into his surroundings—after all, most creatures have an ability to camouflage to some extent. Sometimes you only find the evidence of a

Chupacabra
Chupacabra parguera

creature's presence, never seeing them directly, like the foot prints from Bigfoot or the droppings from mountain lions. We know they are there, but they are just too elusive.

It was as I was finishing the physical exam that he moved. Not much. Just enough movement to give us all a little heart attack. It was moments later that I made my tentative diagnosis. This glorious chupacabra, mythical creature, the most amazing animal I had ever seen, had likely knocked himself unconscious by flying into this little girl's window. Birds do it all the time. They are cruising along and see a window but think it is actually a pass through, a breezeway to the other side of the building. It makes them seem stupid, but birds are actually really smart animals. Arctic terns fly halfway around the world and return to the nest they made the previous spring. A penguin can find its offspring in a colony of tens of thousands. But sadly, hundreds of millions of birds are killed every year by hitting windows so hard that they break their necks because they just don't quite understand the concept of a pane of glass. Sometimes they are stunned and are eaten by predators as they lay unconscious on the ground. You may have seen those hawk-shaped window decals that are intended to prevent such collisions. Well, this little girl's house did not have a chupacabra decal, and my best guess was that this dude hit the glass hard enough to stun himself but not hard enough to break the glass (or his neck). The kid likely heard it while she was lying in bed and went outside to find him.

If you ever have a small bird fly into your window and stun itself, the treatment is often quite simple. You take the bird, put it in a cardboard box and leave it alone for about an hour. This gives him a chance to recover from the "concussion," and then when you open the box, hopefully he flies away to live happily ever after. My dilemma at this point is that I did not have an enormous cardboard box reinforced with kevlar at my disposal. I started telling Alvin my crazy idea that what we needed was a strong box about the size of a small car that we could use to contain and protect the patient (named Cletus by this point) for an hour or so in order for him to get his balance and bearings back. Fortunately for us, the hotel had just had a couple washing machines installed, and the ever-observant Alvin had seen one of the workers haul the boxes over to a trash/recycling area. He ran off and returned quickly with a really thick cardboard box. It would have to do.

The last time I had done this was with an American Robin. They stand about 10 inches tall and weigh less than a quarter pound. I had heard the "thud" of it hitting a window at my house and placed the unconscious bird in a modest-sized cardboard box before a neighborhood cat could find him. When I opened the box an hour later, it came exploding out and into a neighboring tree—easy as pie. As we placed the now wiggling Cletus into the cardboard box, I did not have the same confidence. We closed the box.

Puerto Rico has the nickname *Isla de Encantas*, Island of Dreams. As I looked across the box at my friend Al, I felt that I was in a dream. We'd spent the earlier part of the evening at one of the island's famed bioluminescent bays, where dinoflagellates glow in the water when splashed around. Floating in an ocean illuminated by microscopic organisms had altered our brains a little. I'd fallen in love with this enchanting island and its beaches, frogs, rain forests, citizens, and really amazing coffee.

Back at the box, Cletus was still for a minute or so and then I think he tried to stand but fell over. Then the scrambling started. Scratching. Pawing. It sounded like he was slipping around on the cardboard. Then I heard him sink his claws into it, and then he did it again. The shape of the box seemed to shift and it appeared to get unstable. He was trying to climb the side as if to get to safety. I placed one hand on a built-in handle on the side and one on the top to keep him contained. In retrospect this was really stupid on my part. I had just been examining his awesome talons and imagining him grabbing and killing his prey with them. Now I heard them piercing the cardboard walls as he climbed his way up the side. In terms of his recovery, however, I took this as a good sign.

"It takes a lot of strength and balance to climb," I said to my assistants as I watched his talons jab through the side of the box just missing my fingers. Then he stopped climbing and just hung on to the inside of the box. We waited. I figured that this was standard chupacabra behavior when threatened. A lot of animals do this. Climb to a safe defensible spot and wait on guard. We were whispering now. I'm not sure why because this nocturnal creature probably had fantastic hearing.

"We'll give it 15 minutes and then open." My Spanish was good enough to tell the little girl 15 minutes more. The huge smile on her face showed that she was really enjoying this. I looked at the time on my watch. There was a bit of rustling and fidgeting in the box over the longest 15 minutes of my life, even though I had released wild animals before. In my first two years as a veterinary student, I volunteered an enormous amount of time at the Raptor and Wildlife Rehabilitation Unit associated with the Louisiana State University vet school in Baton Rouge. My bird-loving classmates and I loved it. A steady stream of hawks, owls, herons, crows, pelicans, and even the occasional bald eagle came through the school's hospital. Eagles had just started making their comeback in Louisiana in the mid-1990s, and the first eagle we released exploded out of the carrier and powered off into the sky, flying within eyeshot for a while, shrieking like the madman that he was. It was very satisfying. On the other hand, I recall releasing a Great Horned Owl—a stunning bird to look at. When I opened the carrier, he just casually hopped out. Then he flew about ten feet away in the field, landed gracefully, turned, stared at me, and waited. I didn't know what to do. I knew he could fly. I'd been watching him in the flight cage all week. He glided back and forth effortlessly and was swooping down and killing the rodents that we left for him. We knew he was ready to go free, but there he sat in the field staring me down. I walked slowly away, got in my car and drove home. Not very satisfying.

So here it was. The big moment. I reached with my arms as extended from my body as possible and flipped open the four interlocking tabs making up the top of the large washing machine box. A couple seconds later, he leapt out sending it skidding off to the side. You could feel the wind from his wings as he lifted up, but

I never actually saw him. That silvery, scaly camouflage must have made him nearly invisible in the night sky. Alvin mumbled, "I guess that's why nobody ever sees them."

We walked the little girl back to her house and thanked her. She was really happy. It made me wonder what effect this experience was going to have on her. My friend and I went back to look at the box. What were we going to do? No one was going to believe us when we told them about what happened this evening. As we talked it over, we decided that it was best to keep it to ourselves. If we shared the story, a bunch of crazed people would descend on this little Puerto Rican town. They might even find the chupacabra and trap or kill it. And that would be a shame.

The veterinarian side of me was unsettled. I am trained to diagnose a problem and fix it—or at least do no harm. I'm still not sure what happened that night. I had no experience treating mystical creatures (if that is what this thing was) and I was pretty sure I did not have magical powers. My thoughts drifted to treating a certain very sick young male cat a few years previously that was suffering from life-threatening spasms of its urinary tract. Occasionally male cats get inflammation and crystals in their urinary system and it can make it difficult to pass urine. Their bladder will get huge and painful. It sounds crazy, but these obstructions appear out of nowhere and the next thing you know a cat owner and their vet are making these life and death decisions involving money that the owner may not have. All three parties hate these stressful experiences—especially the cat. And here I was again with a suffering cat and a man without the financial resources (a fair number of people in Buffalo do not have disposable income—it's not a wealthy city) and me just wanting to fix the problem. The cat was not going to survive the night like this, and the guy just could not bring himself to put the cat to sleep. So, I gave the cat a huge dose of a morphine-like medication (so he would not suffer) and gave the owner the phone number of an overnight clinic. I went home feeling lousy about the whole thing and dutifully called the man when I returned to work early the next morning expecting the worst. "How did he do overnight?" I asked. "Fantastic," was the reply. "He peed up a storm all night. He's eating and acting almost like his old self." The cat would go on to live a long life. I do my best. So much is out of my control. There is nothing in the Hippocratic oath about caring for chupacabras.

CHAPTER TWO

BUFFALO IS A QUIRKY TOWN—THERE are characters everywhere. I moved here twenty years ago following my graduation from veterinary school in Baton Rouge for my first real job and it was partly the entertaining people that kept me here.

I met Harold through his wife Jessica. He was a successful businessman and property manager who had lived in Buffalo for decades and knew tons of people. He was active in a number of business, social, and political groups. He and his wife loved horses and, when he decided to cut back on business interests in the city of Buffalo, they were presented with the opportunity to buy a property in the exurbs that included a lovely old farmhouse, a commercial stable, a large riding arena for the horses (which are popular in western New York in the winter), and several hundred acres of hay fields and woods. They bought Marble Ridge Farm and loved it thoroughly.

New York is a diverse state. If you have only been to NYC, you'd never believe the rest of the state was covered in mountains, streams, gorges, glacier-carved lakes, vineyards, and rolling farmland. When I moved here from Louisiana, I never anticipated how much I would enjoy the countryside.

Marble Ridge was everything they hoped it would be. I would visit there regularly in my pickup truck to get free loads of their amazing composted horse manure for our little urban garden. I'd bring my toddler son, check out the horses, ride around the hay fields with Jessica and Harold, and check out the woods that surrounded the property. A lot of New York State is developed, but, as I said, there are places where wild creatures can live. It was in the property's woods where Harold saw the sasquatch. One night around sunset he was running errands around the property. He'd left some carpentry equipment out near the tree line earlier in the day thinking that he would return later to finish the job, but time had run out and it was supposed to rain overnight. As he was loading his equipment into his Gator (a slow-moving six-wheel "four wheeler"), something caught his eye in the woods. He stopped and stared. Probably just a deer. There are tons of deer in the woods out here. But it wasn't a deer. It looked like a man. A really big man. A hairy man. It stopped moving when it realized that it had been spotted. They stared at each other with 30 yards between them.

Harold loved his property and was always taking photos of the fields and horses and people, which meant he had a simple camera in the storage compartment of the Gator. He slowly brought it out, and started taking pictures as the visitor silently walked into the fading light.

If you think I am kidding—I am not. You can see the photos for yourself online. They look almost like the stills from the Patterson film shot in Northern California in 1967. He went home and uploaded the best ones. And then the craziness started. Some people get so wild about sasquatch. Almost immediately after the posting, people began attacking him for trying to create a hoax. Some guy even claimed that he had seen Harold purchasing a gorilla suit at a Halloween store the previous week. Harold was quoted in the local paper saying that he never wanted this attention. He was a respected businessman and all he did was post a photo. People just needed to calm down. In retrospect, it was really naive to not expect people to freak out. I think he kind of expected some attention but doubt that he anticipated the personal attacks. He wasn't used to people questioning his honesty, and he certainly did not expect articles in the largest local paper questioning his motives.

What he most certainly did not expect was several hundred cryptozoologists, both professional and amateur, descending on his little piece of paradise. Again, this really happened! They came out of nowhere. They came in vans, carrying cameras, night vision goggles, and listening devices. These people were nuts. They trespassed. They knocked down fences, cut wires, scared his horses, trampled his fields, and annoyed the people who were boarding their horses at the stables. All because of this remarkably cool photo that has still, *to this day*, not been disproved. I never doubted the photo or his story for a second, because I had met a distant relative of his visitor in the woods behind my parents' house outside Shreveport, Louisiana when I was a teenager. And my introduction to a sasquatch was way more intimate than that of my friend Harold.

Moving to Shreveport was refreshing for me as a sixteen-year-old. I am an Army Brat and have lived in a number of places. My father was a gynecologist in the service, and I was born in an Army hospital on Okinawa during the Vietnam War. We lived in San Antonio and then El Paso, Texas before moving to Louisiana. In El Paso, we lived on the edge of town halfway up the Franklin Mountains. I am the last of four children and, by the time I was a teenager, my parents had become very relaxed about keeping tabs on their youngest child. My older siblings are several years older than me and they also kind of looked after me. This meant that my friends and I had access to the neighborhood and endless surrounding desert where we could hike, bike, climb cliffs, look for snakes and tarantulas, chase road runners, and try to catch bats in flight. (It's not possible, we tried really hard.)

But as a kid who was fascinated with nature, moving to northwest Louisiana blew my mind. My parents bought a house on a modest lot on the western end of Shreveport. The neighborhood abutted Cross Lake, a good-sized lake ringed with cypress trees that could pass for a postcard. But the best part was that our home backed on to several hundred acres of uninhabited north Louisiana woods and waterways, and I just about lost my mind exploring. It took me a while to sort it out, but this property had been a working farm a few decades before. It turns out that, when the patriarch of the farming family died decades earlier, a family feud started and the property went into receivership. The property had been fought over by the heirs for years and as a result had fallen into decay. But the upside of the neglect was that nature had reclaimed the area and wildlife flourished.

For me, it was heaven. There were old dirt roads all over the property and abandoned fields that had become meadows or groves of bamboo. There were ponds full of fish, turtles and frogs where they had once watered their livestock. There were several houses with barns and greenhouses. But most importantly, there was nature. I saw water moccasins and alligators, and alligator snapping turtles, foxes, and deer. The far end of it even had a rookery for egrets with thousands of white birds nesting in the cypress trees high above the water. We would paddle our canoes and *pirogues* (that's a Cajun kayak) around the trees looking at the chicks above and trying to spy the lurking alligators as they waited for a meal of failed fledgling.

A few months after moving there, my older brother, Brad moved back in with us after finishing his job on an Arabian horse farm in west Texas. We were in complete agreement—this place was for us. We were far enough out of town that we could see the stars at night and listen to the barred owls call to each other when

Barred Owl
Strix varia

the tree frogs did not drown them out. We had really friendly neighbors, and the next thing I knew we were helping to care for a couple horses belonging to a neighbor my brother met. Access to horses only added to my ability to explore and survey my kingdom. We cleared brush and built horse jumps from fallen trees. We dug "canals" off the pond for water obstacles. We camped, fished, hung hammocks high in the pine trees, rolled in the mud, swam in the murky water, listened to the birds, stargazed and soaked in the solitude. When I showed my brother the farm's old greenhouses, he was overjoyed. He had briefly majored in horticulture and loved to grow just about anything. The greenhouse had some of the richest soil you could find. Just imagine that a farmer had built and managed this space as the incubator for his livelihood and then it sat empty for a couple decades. We started in on the gardening the same day my brother learned of the greenhouse. I was his apprentice. We dug and tilled and weeded and planted and watered for hours. This was going to be amazing— carrots, tomatoes, peas, herbs, and so much more! We checked it every day and awaited the harvest.

We loved walking the woods at night and did it almost every evening. It was especially good when the moon was out. We loved those woods and all the exotic creatures, and would wander around trying to triangulate where the owls were roosting based on their calls. We'd bring flashlights, but not because we needed them. We knew every trail and twist in the woods. We'd use them to light up the eyes of the animals we came across. The best part of the game was trying to figure out if it was a deer or a fox or a raccoon. The coolest eyes we found were the alligators floating in the lake and ponds. It was an almost prehistoric feeling.

The woods could get a little spooky sometimes knowing that there were snakes and alligators all over. We just never knew what we would run into at night. One time, one of the neighboring fences must have come down and a creature ventured in to graze around on all the fresh pasture. We saw him from a good ways off one night. It scared the hell out of us. We kept our distance, studying him, trying to figure out what this enormous four-legged, slow-moving creature in the tall grass was. We snuck closer. He did not seem intimidated by us and then, ever so slowly, he raised his big bovine head. Pretty cool. We did not expect to find a cow in our woods.

The following night we were out making our rounds again. We had not been to the greenhouse in a couple days and made our way there with purpose to check on our crops. We always walked quietly and listened. As we approached the greenhouse, we heard a crash. That damn cow had found our secret garden! You can imagine what a twelve-hundred-pound cow can do to a garden. We were pissed but also a little afraid of the cow. Most cows are generally docile but some breeds are kind of nuts. My brother knew this from his time on the horse farm. We were going to scare the hell out of this cow, but we were going to do it carefully. We made our plans. Brad was in charge. I was going to follow his lead. I felt like I was preparing for combat duty. We'd just watched the first *Terminator* movie together the night before. We were going to be cow commandos!

Thinking it was a cow was reasonable. We were so wrong. My brother and I stealthily approached our violated greenhouse. Our anticipation was huge. We could hear the creature moving around inside and could hear the chomping. I can still hear the crunching sounds to this day. As we approached the dirty glass and struggled to look through, we could see a large shape inside. My brother gave a cool hand signal as if he was a platoon leader and we silently shifted over a couple steps to look through a broken pane. As I stared in, my first instinct was to run and I would have if not for my brother holding me back. Squatting in our rich soil was an enormous hairy primate chowing down on our carrots. He was pulling out entire clusters by the greens, shaking off the dirt and munching them down casually.

Sasquatch
Dinanthropoides magnipus

I was a pretty confident nature-boy at this point. Snakes, alligators, tarantulas, horses, snapping turtles were all just part of my life. I had seen a lot in my brief life and I had good composure when interacting with strange and scary animals. Once, when I was ten, I got to wrestle with a tiger cub at the El Paso zoo where my mother was a docent. But nothing prepares you for standing twenty feet from Bigfoot. This dude was huge and he looked exactly like you would expect—just like the sketches and the creature from *Harry and the Hendersons*. He was spectacular, like a lanky gorilla with dreadlocks. We stared, amazed and terrified. This thing could break us like twigs. I motioned to my brother that we needed to get out of here. He nodded, and then, as we started to slowly back away, the creature looked up and sniffed the air. We were so screwed. Sneaking around in the woods at night had seemed like such an exciting idea. All we could do now was silently stare at this enormous beast as it sniffed for our scent and started looking around. Eventually he looked our way and locked on to us. Once he started looking, I knew we were going to be found out. As we looked into each other's faces, I had the stupid teenaged impulse to shine my flashlight into his face to see whether his retinas would brightly reflect like so many nocturnal creatures do. Do sasquatch have a *tapetum lucidum*? Always a scientist—even back then. I was always looking for tests and data. My brother firmly grabbed my wrist as I raised my flashlight and gave me an "are you insane?" look. Totally appropriate. It was then that the creature stood up and backed away from us and moved toward the door. I guess sasquatch are not carnivores. If they were, we would both be dead. He just walked off into the night with a couple handfuls of our vegetables. We waited, on an incredible adrenaline high, then we started home with real purpose. Not speaking, but listening intently. I still expected that beast to jump out of the woods at any second. We made it home and locked all the doors. We were freaking out.

As chance would have it, I had pranked my brother the day before. It had rained earlier in the day and when I went walking in the woods, I was barefoot. I thought it would be funny to do a slip and slide and skip gait when I walked through a muddy section of trail. The effect was to make what looked like elongated human footprints that resembled what a sasquatch print might look like. I really nailed it. They looked great. What I did not know was that my brother actually saw the prints once the mud dried. My brother has an active imagination. He was starting to suspect that we might have a sasquatch in the woods even before that fateful night.

Turns out that we did have a sasquatch, but what could we do about it? I have to admit that I was really scared for a few days. That thing could rip your house apart and tear you into pieces if it wanted to. But it didn't. In fact, I never saw it again, although I did see evidence of his presence. For instance, he ate the whole damn garden the next night. I saw prints around from time to time. They were hard to find. I was certain that this creature was aware of the threat that being discovered would present. He would never step in the mud. He walked in the grass, trying to leave no traces. I'm pretty sure I found his scat. I started reading up on how to be a tracker. I got better at it but was nothing special.

Most amusingly, I learned that sasquatch really love marijuana. My stoner neighbor Roger got the bright idea that he could grow his weed in the woods—a clever idea actually (and something practiced by drug cartels). There was a lot of space in our woods, and most of it was off the beaten path. He had some seeds left over and planted them in a few different spots. The weed thrived of course. But when the marijuana plants started to reach maturity, someone pulled them up. This happened over and over until Roger blamed me knowing that I spent so much time in the woods. He was pissed that his lovely organic stash was being destroyed. But how could I tell him that it was my beast friend that was eating his crop?

I learned much later that cryptozoologists suspect that sasquatch really like cannabis. In certain parts of the south, people refer to their sub-species as a Skunk Ape. I presumed that this is based on their body odor. Maybe they do smell bad, or maybe they just smell like their favorite food: marijuana. I like to think that our sasquatch was a little high when my brother and I ruined his raid on the greenhouse. He was certainly very chill about our intrusion that night.

When I learned of Harold's sasquatch sighting in suburban Buffalo, all these memories came flooding back to me. I called my brother, who was living in Washington DC by then, and he flew up to Buffalo the next weekend. We reminisced about our experiences twenty years before in the woods near Shreveport and we went to go visit Harold and Jessica on their farm. It was under the pretense that my brother loved horses—which he does to this day. After a couple glasses of wine, I brought up their recent sasquatch sighting. My friends responded by acting a little annoyed. Who could blame them? They had experienced enough mocking for a lifetime and the sasquatch "hunters" had actually wrecked a couple fences on their property that very day. My brother and I related our story about seeing a similar creature in the woods behind our parents' house years ago. They could see that we were serious as we started to share the details of our experiences. Frankly, it was great to discuss this amazing experience we shared, and actually not have my sanity questioned. We really bonded and they eventually took us on a "Sasquatch Tour" of the farm. It made my brother and me happy to be out in the woods again looking for mischief, knowing that there were at least a few of these guys still out there.

As a veterinarian who has worked in wildlife rehabilitation, I was amazed that this enormous creature persisted in our heavily-populated and heavily-armed country. They must be remarkably crafty. So many animals have been pushed to the brink by habitat destruction, pesticides, hunting, and more. What I did not realize at the time was that this very credible sasquatch sighting had brought a poacher to our community. The poachers of mystical creatures are a ruthless and sophisticated bunch. I'm sure that you are aware that illegal hunting is alive and well on this planet. People poach elephants, rhinos, whales and more. The more endangered the creature, the more valuable the trophies. Ask yourself: If an elephant tusk is worth tens of thousands of dollars, then what would an intact Bigfoot be worth? Apparently somewhere on the Dark Web a poacher had found himself a credible buyer willing to pay top dollar for our sasquatch. He'd set up camp out in the woods on the fringes of my friend's farm and was waiting.

Nobody knows the exact details of what happened the night the sasquatch was shot, but here is what Harold and I were able to piece together. Just after dusk on a warm evening, a shot was heard in the woods not far from where the sasquatch was first sighted. I had not been searching this part of the woods following the first sighting as I had figured that once the creature was discovered he would move on. But apparently something kept him to this area. I have wondered if one of Harold's neighbors was growing cannabis on the side because they seemed to be drawn to the stuff. Anyway, the poacher's rifle shot hit the sasquatch but not fatally. As the beast struggled to get away from danger, he made his way toward one of the trails where a boarder happened to be riding his horse. (This is where this animal tale starts to sound like *America's Most Wanted*.) The guy riding the horse happened to be an officer for the NYS Department of Environmental Conservation. In Louisiana, we would call him a Game Warden. The guy was a long-time friend of Jessica and Harold and was out enjoying an evening with his horse. DEC officers are armed most of the time and, of course, his senses were heightened by the sound of the rifle shot. In amazement, the officer watched as this huge and hairy "guy" stumbled out onto the trail clearly wounded. In pursuit, out steps the poacher and they start aiming their weapons at each other. They each tell the other to drop their weapons and mind their own business. Eventually the poacher backs away. I guess he decided that he did not want to be a murderer of humans, especially a law enforcement officer.

When Harold was led to the wounded sasquatch, he did what any sensible person would do. He called his friend the veterinarian, the same veterinarian who days before had been relating his own experiences with a sasquatch. At first, I thought they were pranking me. Why not? Everyone had been giving them a hard time. Why not pass it around? It was Friday night. It would not be the first time a friend had called me with an animal question or request at an odd time. But it soon became clear that they were very serious. As chance would have it, one of my neighbors is also a vet, and an exotic animal vet at that. I called Jack as I jumped in my truck.

"There's a large injured exotic animal at my friend's farm and I really need your help," I said.

"What kind of animal?" he asked.

"You won't believe me 'til you see it," I replied.

That was all he needed to hear. The weirder the better. I picked him up at his front door moments later. He even had his medical treatment travel bag. What a guy!

The drive to the farm took a while as I live in north Buffalo near the historic Delaware Park. On the way, I filled in Dr. Jack Anderson that the patient we were speeding to see was likely the sasquatch that had been in the news last week. I told him that it had been shot by a poacher and that it was likely to be in bad shape. Jack was horrified to hear that some jerk had shot a sasquatch, but exhilarated to be rushing to the crime scene. This was going to be the night of his life. He peppered me with a ton of questions, most of which I could not answer. The most important question he had was: What are we going to do with him? He's huge and had likely lost a lot of blood. That's when I suggested calling the vet for the Buffalo Zoo. Jack had worked at the Buffalo Zoo intermittently as an assistant vet for years, and I had volunteered at the Zoo a little, helping out when they were raising funds to renovate their old hospital. If we were going to save a gun shot sasquatch, we needed Dr. Victor and his hospital. He had a modern hospital following the expansion and no one else in town had cages that could handle a sasquatch.

Jack called him from my truck. At first, Dr. Kyle Victor thought Jack was joking with him when he gave him the low down, but Jack persisted.

"No, I have not been drinking," he said. "No, I don't think you're stupid."

Dr. Victor had heard about the sasquatch out in the 'burbs of Buffalo and, when I got on the phone to confirm the story, he decided this may actually be real. Kyle also lived near the zoo and was going to keep his cell phone handy for an update from the crime scene.

As we raced through the Buffalo suburbs, I started to think that my life had taken a turn for the weird. It was only a few weeks ago that I had stood in the Puerto Rican night administering aid to a what I now strongly suspected was a chupacabra. Since the incident, I had spent a lot of time reading about cryptozoology. It's a fascinating subject—so much folklore and history, with interesting biology to boot! For ages, people speculated that the giant squid did not actually exist: until we found them. Giant pandas, Komodo dragons, mountain gorillas, coelacanths—none of these creatures seemed possible until they were finally discovered. After my sasquatch exposure as a kid, it had all seemed possible. I read about mermaids, centaurs, griffons, jackalopes, and more—knowing that these strange creatures may actually exist. Was destiny drawing me to these mystical creatures? One thing was for sure, if we were going to save this sasquatch, it was going to take more than placing him in a cardboard box and waiting.

By the time we reached the farm, Harold and Jessica and his officer friend had managed to get this unconscious primate on to the Gator and drive him into the entry of the riding arena. Dr. Anderson and I proceeded to start assessing the patient. There appeared to be a single bullet entry in the back just below his shoulder blade with a clean exit out near his armpit. He'd lost a fair bit of blood but his color and vitals were OK. He was unconscious and looked exactly like the one I had seen in my youth except that I suspect that this one was a little smaller. Maybe he was an adolescent sasquatch. We were thankful that he was not full-sized as we transferred him to the bed of my pickup for the ride back to town. My friends at the farm were visibly angry. As much trouble as this creature had caused them, he was spectacular and they could not believe that someone had the nerve to come on to their property to try to kill him. The DEC officer was the calmest of the bunch. In his line of work, he'd seen gunshot wounds before. We thanked him for stepping in and potentially saving this guy's life. He joked about tracking the poacher down for hunting Bigfoot without the proper permits and then said that he thought the actual damage might not be that bad, but that there was certainly some internal bleeding.

Dr. Anderson stayed in the truck bed with the patient. (He'd named him Harry almost immediately.) We wrapped him up in a horse blanket to keep him warm and cover him up a little, and then started toward the zoo. As excited as I was, I drove exactly the speed limit. I did not want to get pulled over. How to explain this one to Officer Friendly? Dr. Anderson called Dr. Victor and gave him the summary. He would be waiting for us at the Zoo's gate off Amherst Street nearest the vet hospital entrance. Everything was open and on when we arrived. He had even called his trusted veterinary technician Anna Roberts, an amazing technician I had met years ago while doing greyhound dog rescue. Veterinary technicians are my profession's version of a registered nurse. Anna had been at the Zoo for decades and she could do it all—radiographs, sedation, restraint, blood work, treatments. She'd been indispensable to Dr. Victor, and we were grateful to have her tonight.

I backed into the loading bay and we pulled Harry onto the scale—220 kilograms! The scale was on wheels and we rolled him into the ICU/treatment room. I have already made the point that wildlife medicine and zoo medicine are hard because they are often uncharted. We do the best we can and try to use common sense. Over the years, veterinarians have learned some hard lessons— Tylenol is lethal in cats, don't give collies ivermectin, the list goes on. We quickly agreed that Dr. Victor was in charge since he was the expert and this was his hospital. We were going to treat Harry as if he were an orangutan.

He was cold—temperature 96 degrees F—so we placed him in some electric warming blankets. Anna started by shaving and cleaning the wounds. Jack had kept pressure on the wounds the whole ride in and the external bleeding had stopped. We inspected the cleaned entry and exit sites and thought they looked decent. They could have been much worse. We speculated on the caliber of the bullet. This one was likely small and hopefully had not done too much damage. Presumably the poacher had chosen a bullet that would be unlikely to blow his trophy to smithereens. Before I realized what had happened, Dr. Victor had an IV catheter in his uninjured arm's wrist and was giving him a shock dose of warmed saline. My colleague was amazing! I took inspiration and started to concentrate better. We needed chest radiographs to see what the damage was. Dr. Anderson and I went to start up the new digital X-ray machine as Kyle talked about transfusions. Transfusions are commonly used in human medicine to replace the components of blood that have been lost. We use them in veterinary medicine, too, but not nearly as commonly. Red blood cells, platelets, clotting factors, plasma, whole blood—they can be life savers. The problem was that we did not have an appropriate donor (duh?) and, if we did, who knows how to blood type a sasquatch?! Maybe one of us could donate a pint of blood? That seemed logical but a little crazy in hindsight. Certainly, the creature would react to a human blood transfusion and we could not risk it. What we did have was a hetastarch. Hetastarch is a synthetic colloidal blood product that expands the plasma portion of your blood. It's useful for treating shock associated with trauma and blood loss. The hospital had a couple bags on hand and Kyle started in on the calculations for an appropriate dose, again presuming that we had your run of the mill large primate before us. We started a continuous blood pressure monitor and the readings were on the low end of normal. That was OK with us, given the circumstances.

In the meantime, Jack had taken a couple radiographs of his chest. The scapula (shoulder blade) was unharmed, one of the ribs was broken (but not too bad), and there was only modest bleeding into the pleural space around his lungs. Miraculously, the bullet had passed clear through. We might save this guy after all! Our technician pointed out that this looked painful to her which prompted Kyle to draw up a sizable dose of an opiate named buprenorphine. This was an easy calculation as he had just done a sedated dental procedure on one of the Zoo's gorillas the previous week under the guidance of our local veterinary dental specialist.

It was at about this time that we all started getting messages from our spouses. We had basically dropped everything and run off to save this guy. We'd done this sort of thing before, and we kind of told the truth: "Sick patient at work. Be home as soon as I can." Then we returned to the patient. He seemed stable enough. We were rehydrating him (we'd checked that he was male), warming him, improving his blood pressure, controlling his pain (that had to really hurt) and, as we discussed it, noted that he would likely get an infection from this bullet. It had certainly dragged some dirty hair right through him. He needed antibiotics and they had to be long acting. He was almost surely really smart, but I doubt that we could teach him to take a pill every 24 hours. Fortunately, there was a new cephalosporin antibiotic on the market that stayed at a therapeutic level for over two weeks. It was only licensed for dogs—which meant that dogs (not even cats) were the only species that had been tested for safety and efficacy. It had not been tested on humans or other primates. It had definitely not been tested on sasquatch, but it was still our best option.

So if we were able to stabilize him and keep him alive, what then? Wildlife rehabilitators face this dilemma all the time. It rarely makes sense to save a creature if you cannot release them back into the wild and have a healthy animal who can eventually take care of himself. So we decided to consider the best possible outcome and plan accordingly.

1. We were able to keep this secret among ourselves—the four of us medical types and the few people at the farm. There would be minimal traffic in the Zoo's vet hospital over the weekend and Dr. Victor could always lock the doors and make up some quarantine story. Quarantines at an exotic animal facility generally scare people away.
2. Harry continues to recover quickly and our restraints can contain him. The injuries associated with gunshots are highly variable, but this one appeared less traumatic than some. As for the "kennel," it should not be a problem as the walls and doors of the facility were rather robust.
3. We can safely transport him back to the woods where we found him. We certainly can't release him in urban Buffalo. We would have to use sedatives to get him back into the truck for transport back to the farm. Fortunately, there are some nice injectable sedatives that we could give him via a dart, and they even have a reversal agent that you can give when you want him to start waking up.

And that was pretty much what happened. It was Friday night when we admitted him into the hospital. We continued to keep him on the warming blankets that we could control from several feet away via a thermostat. We gave him intravenous fluids and hetastarch until we felt he was rehydrated and then we waited. We cared for him in pairs (so that our spouses would not be too suspicious that we disappeared for an entire weekend). Early on Saturday, he started to awaken. The first thing he did was pull out the IV catheter. When he woke up enough to realize that he was in a cage, he backed into the corner to survey the situation. He never freaked out or tried to break anything. When Jack returned for his shift on Saturday morning, he brought about a half gallon of blueberries from a local grocery and Harry ate them almost immediately. Turns out that he liked peanut butter too. By late Saturday night, we were planning his return to the farm for the next day.

The barn had a separate section of stalls where I thought we could wake him up from anesthesia. Knowing the typical barn, we knew that a wooden stall could not fully contain this guy, but if he woke quickly and broke out of the stall, then walked off across the field and into the woods, that was OK. We started our planning. Veterinarians (like most people in medicine) have to be good at preparation and contingency planning. It's probably more important for zoo vets like Dr. Victor. You don't get a lot of extra time when you are dealing with, say, a hippopotamus. You need to be ready for just about anything. Unexpected problems happen, and they happen quickly. I recalled one of my experiences from my fourth year of vet school. I was training at a lovely zoo in south Texas with Dr. Melissa Ford. She was always prepared. My first impression of her was that she was uptight. I was wrong. She was actually just really smart and had learned from her experiences. One morning, we were going to sedate a juvenile baboon for a wellness exam before transferring him to his new home at a zoo in north Texas. She walked me through the sedation (with a dart gun), maintaining the patient on gas anesthesia, his physical exam, the blood draw for tests and which were the best veins, and how and where we were going to wake him up. Dr. Ford had done similar procedures and she hammered into my head how we were going to be ready for every imaginable possibility. I was in charge of keeping the baboon properly anesthetized using a light dose of gas anesthesia via a face mask. Can you imagine if he started waking up and we could not control him? The hardest part was not getting caught up in the wonder of looking at the beautiful baboon: his teeth, nose, markings, skull, muscles. Fortunately, it went well that day and there were no surprises.

So, on Sunday afternoon it was time. Harry was alert, eating regularly and looking like he had formulated a plan to break out of this joint. Clearly this was a smart animal to survive in western New York for years without being discovered. He was not fully recovered from the gun shot but we thought he could make it on his own. Our DEC officer friend had actually located a tracking collar left over from a project with the NYS Fish and Wildlife Department. We figured that we could slip that on him while he was sedated. We knew that he would tear it off at some point but we felt better knowing that we could track him for a while.

We started at 4 p.m. Marble Ridge Stables was closed to boarders due to "emergency reconstruction" of the hay loft. No one would be allowed on the property as not to interfere with the efforts of the "carpenters." Dr. Victor had chosen a sedating combination using medetomidine and ketamine, and we would be dosing him like he was an orangutan. Both medications are commonly used with primates and, most importantly, both are reversible. We darted him from outside the cage and waited for it to take effect. Although it seemed to take forever, it took about five minutes for him to look drowsy. We moved in cautiously, fearful that he was not fully sedated. As we all strained to lift him to a gurney, Jack was checking out the entry and exit wounds. They looked to be healing well. He applied triple antibiotic ointment and attached bandages to both wounds. Then it was into Dr. Victor's truck, with a covered bed this time, and we were off. We would be cutting it close. Marble Ridge was a 35-minute drive from the Zoo and this anesthetic protocol should last 40-45 minutes. As a precaution, we brought along a portable gas anesthesia machine so that we could keep him sedated if he started to wake up—again, contingency plans. We placed the tracking device on his ankle during the drive. Dr. Victor drove exactly the speed limit and we arrived without incident at a near empty stable. As we transferred him to the waiting Gator, he was starting to wake up. Anesthesia is as much an art as it is a science. One of my favorite professors in vet school, an anesthesiologist, had a poster on her wall that read: "Anesthesiology—hours of boredom spiced with moments of panic." And almost panic was what I did when Harry grabbed Jack's arm as we were backing the Gator into the stall. This dude was waking up a couple minutes ahead of schedule and that would be OK as long as we could get Harry to let go. His hand would eventually release Jack's arm but it took a lot of prying and coaxing. It made us wonder just how strong this guy would be if he was conscious. It was something we did not want to find out.

Anna administered the reversal agent as we transferred him onto the Gator. It would take a few minutes to work, but hopefully things would start happening quickly. We laid him down into the hay of the horse stall and closed the doors. To our luck, the stables had been fitted with security cameras a few months earlier. Harold, the tech savvy owner of the stables, had spent the morning relocating a couple of the cameras so that we were able to watch the stall, the entrance to the stall, the hallway, and the outside of the barn leading to his home in the woods where he had been shot days before.

We went to the tack room to watch the monitors and wait. Almost immediately he started moving his arms then lifting his head. It was oddly like watching my feline patients recover. Eventually he sat up and tried to stand up but fell into the soft hay. This went on for almost an hour until he got his balance and started to try to figure a way out of the stall which was closed from the outside. We had decided that we would let him get as awake as the stall could handle. We wanted him to be able to fend for himself. The farm was near the intersection of two roads, and we didn't want him to leave the stall so confused that he wandered along the road and was spotted—or worse. Eventually, it was time to let him go. Jessica had rigged a rope to the stall door latch, and, when she pulled (from well around the corner), the door slid open. It was just past dusk. We had timed it perfectly. It took a minute or two, but eventually he cautiously stepped out of the stall and started towards the open door at the end of the short hallway. He was moving rather well for someone who had been shot 48 hours earlier. As he stepped out the door, he looked out across the hay fields and into the woods where he had been spotted twice. We watched eagerly, expecting him make his way toward his "home." Instead, he took an abrupt left and walked along the barn and headed across the street and up the driveway of a neighbor. Oh no! What had we done? We had binoculars (of course, preparations!) and could see that the house was occupied. In fact, we could see the elderly couple who lived there inside watching *Wheel of Fortune*. Fortunately, they were caught up in Pat and Vanna's latest puzzle and did not see this enormous creature walk down their driveway, past their house and into the neighboring woods. Maybe people these days are just too caught up in their own worlds to notice the interesting things around them.

And that was the last time we saw him. We followed his tracker for days. That evening he walked another few hundred yards and apparently laid down in a secluded spot in the woods and slept off the medications. We rotated our surveillance duties and each of the four of us spent the next two days following his signal as he foraged around in the woods near the farm. Then the signal stopped moving. He either tore it off or he was in need of our help. We met at the barn just before dawn and tried to be prepared for anything. Gator, dart gun, medications, reversal agents, everything we could think of. We also brought our DEC policeman friend as back up, and also because the guy was really good at navigating the woods. We followed the signal for about a quarter mile until we found the tracking device. He'd pulled it off and gone off to live his sasquatch life. On the way back to the farm, we talked about this magical experience we'd had, and I reflected on my vet school days as a wildlife rehabber. This was a success. We'd returned a healthy animal back to his habitat. Hopefully he'll stay out of trouble, find a lady sasquatch, and have a bunch of sasquatch babies.

CHAPTER THREE

D O YOU BELIEVE IN COINCIDENCE? I always have, but this was getting weird. These last two experiences had truly freaked me out. Don't get me wrong. I loved every moment of it, but this made me start to believe that strange forces were at work. I began to wonder why we end up leading the lives that we do, and reflected on my father who had recently passed away. In many ways, my father and I were similar people, so much so that my siblings still call me "Xerox." Certainly, he had instilled in me the values and work ethic that inspired my veterinary career, although you could argue that my mother's adoration of animals played an equal role.

My father, Warren, was born in a small town in Wisconsin the week of the 1929 stock market collapse that led to the Great Depression. Despite the world-wide economic chaos, his father, mother, and older sister lived a comfortable life in Hudson, a small town along the St. Croix River where my grandfather worked as manager of a cheese factory. (This was Wisconsin after all.) My grandfather's grandparents had left Norway in the early 1870s to escape a series of famines. At the time, Norway was not the idyllic country we know today but was a virtual serfdom where the average person could not own land. Life there was terrible for most people, and so, like a lot of Europeans of that era, my ancestors sought a better life. So, my great, great grandpa went first to Hamburg, Germany, and on to America via an ocean liner. Most Norwegians arriving in America landed in New York City, travelled right through the Northeast, often through Buffalo, and settled in the Midwest and upper plains.

When my father was four, his father died suddenly from a heart attack—too much cream, my father would joke to us kids. My grandmother converted their large home in downtown Hudson into a boarding house and survived the Great Depression with a lot of help from her oldest daughter, Audrey. My father told us many stories of an enjoyable childhood that sounded a little like Huck Finn's. He went ice-skating on, and swimming in, the St. Croix River, and spent summers near Minot, North Dakota working on his Uncle Pearl's farm. Pearl was one of the Norwegian bachelor farmers that Garrison Keillor writes about in his *Lake Wobegon Days*. Uncle Pearl could see that his nephew was bright, industrious, and a little mischievous, and the two formed a life-long bond.

When my father was a senior in high school, he met with his guidance counselor (also the school principal in this small town) who knew very well that my dad was raised in poverty by a single mother. The principal was a little shocked when the young man told him that he wanted to go to medical school, and he steered him away from such a lofty goal. "There's no shame in good, honest labor, son," my father used to quote his principal's words to us. My dad agreed with the sentiment. He had done honest labor on his uncle's farm, but that life just wasn't for him. His afterschool job during high school had been mowing the rather hilly local cemetery with an un-motorized push mower. This drudgery may have convinced him that he wanted to be a scientist and help people. His childhood hero was the cowboy movie star Gene Autry. My father also wanted to see the world. As a child, he had often told his mother and sister that he wanted to "Go West." This was figurative of course, but represented that he wanted somewhere, and something, bigger.

With financial help from Pearl and a lot of part-time jobs during college and medical school, my father fulfilled his dream and graduated from the University of Wisconsin medical school in Madison. He would be drafted into the Army and serve in Korea, work as a small town doctor in rural Wisconsin, and eventually join the Army (on his own free will this time). In the Army, he would complete a residency, become a gynecologist, and be stationed in the Pacific Ocean on the island of Okinawa, where his youngest son—that would be me—was born. Okinawa was my father's paradise. After decades of study and toil, he was living with his family in a tropical paradise and doing the work that he loved. Okinawa has many lovely beaches and he spent every possible free moment at the beach with us. I don't recall learning how to swim. My family tells me that I started swimming in the ocean as soon as I could walk.

When I finished my own medical education at LSU-SVM, I interviewed at a number of veterinary practices across the country where I could work with just cats. I love all animals, but I had decided that cat medicine was going to be the best for me. They are the perfect-sized patients, and I have long-adored their personalities and wild nature. When I traveled to interview at a feline-only practice in Buffalo, New York, I must admit that I was rather ignorant about what the region had to offer—other than the infamous snow storms. I quickly learned about the wineries, gorges and other amenities, but it was Lake Erie that fascinated me. By this time in my life, I had traveled a fair bit and had seen the ocean in Texas, Hawaii, Atlantic Canada, and Scotland, but what was this "ocean" doing in upstate New York? If you have never seen one of the Great Lakes, they almost don't look real because of their size. With all five of them, you generally can't see the other side. Lake Erie is the smallest of the Great Lakes, and even it has over 125 trillion gallons of water. The Lakes contain twenty percent of the world's fresh surface water. On windy days, the waves rise to eight feet or more and it really looks like an ocean.

I settled in Buffalo, New York and began to explore the countryside and waterways. I was fortunate that the owner of the practice had a good friend who was an avid sailor. My sailing experience was limited at that point, but I was eager to learn. Madeline Winthrop, the owner and captain of a 29-foot sailboat, was part of an active sailboat racing club and she put me to work. I learned how to raise the sails, trim them, operate the helm, plot courses, read the wind and more. I am an agile and somewhat fearless person so I was often lifted by the main halyard up to the top of the mast in a bosun's harness (the sailing version of a zipline harness). As a teenager, I spent a lot of time climbing trees and jumping off roofs into neighborhood pools. At one point, I hung a hammock about sixty feet up a pine tree in the woods behind my parents' house. I used to read books and nap up there when I needed solitude. This was clearly reckless adolescent behavior, but my need for excitement would continue into adulthood. My fondest memories of sailing are being placed out on the rail in heavy weather to balance the boat. I loved the excitement of sailboat racing and continued even after my friend retired from racing.

I was sailing on another friend's boat when I met Dennis Ferdinand, a seasoned sailor and a real character. We hit it off and started trading stories. When people find out that you are a veterinarian, they generally want to tell you stories about their pets—whether you want to hear them or not. We eventually started talking about the fish of the Great Lakes. I discovered that Dennis was a biologist in the Wildlife and Fisheries Department and had been working on a project to study the health of lake sturgeon, *Acipenser fulvescens*, in Lake Erie.

Before I continue, though, I should tell you more about my circuitous path to becoming a veterinarian. My first degree was a bachelors in Mechanical Engineering from Louisiana Tech University near my parents' home in Shreveport. I have always loved the sciences and had thoughts of being an aeronautical engineer when I happened to see a flyer one night of my senior year while walking through the science building on campus. It advertised getting a master's degree in Ocean Physics at Memorial University of Newfoundland (MUN) in St. John's, Newfoundland, Canada. The photo of the shoreline was beautiful, and this sounded like a really cool field of science to study and a great adventure. I would spend three years studying physics and oceanography while living in one of the most beautiful places in North America. Newfoundland has so much to offer—icebergs, seals, moose, caribou, fjords, ancient Viking and Basque settlements, rivers of salmon. I loved my time spent there in classrooms, nature, and on research vessels. Upon completion of my master's degree, I returned to Louisiana to study veterinary medicine.

When he learned of my diverse educational experience, Dennis invited me to volunteer with him on board one of the state research vessels. They had been catching sturgeon and studying their reproductive health. I had no idea that the Great Lakes even had sturgeon, but it makes sense. These lakes are huge, ancient, and fertile. I jumped at the opportunity to get back on a research vessel. The crew did not really need me, but I knew I would not get in the way and hoped that I might actually be helpful. Being an engineer, oceanographer, and veterinary surgeon had to count for something.

Lake Erie is the shallowest of the Great Lakes. It's several hundred miles long from Buffalo to almost Detroit, Michigan, but only 210 feet at its deepest. For comparison, Lake Superior, the largest Great Lake, is 1330 feet deep and has 3 quadrillion gallons of water. Regardless of size, each of the Great Lakes contains ancient fish including a sturgeon species similar to the Russian one that yields the famous caviar. The Great Lakes have been under enormous stress from people for two centuries—invasive species, sewage, storm water and industrial run off, fertilizer from farms, tributary destruction, overfishing, tens of millions of people living in its watershed, and, of course, climate change. Fishing has long been a huge industry on the Lakes. At the end of the nineteenth century, sturgeon eggs and meat became prized, and the species was fished to near extinction. In 2001, the regional fish and wildlife departments thankfully started reintroduction programs and scientists like Dennis have been monitoring the sturgeon population and its recovery.

I met the crew at dawn one morning at the Great Lakes Center on Buffalo's harbor. I had passed the Center countless times on my way to the yacht club and was a little surprised by the small size of the research vessel for the day, a 27-foot, mostly-open boat called the Friedhoff. It was a state-of-the-art vessel, but was actually smaller than the sailboats I had been racing on. While in grad school in Newfoundland, I had been fortunate to have a professor who was very serious about collecting data. Temperature, salinity, current—Dr. Ben deYorg and I were often at sea deploying equipment and retrieving it months later. I loved being out on the North Atlantic, and over those three years, I had been on numerous Canadian research ships. They were all way bigger than this one. (As an aside, I would later learn that the current vessel was named for Captain John Friedhoff, who'd been the lead captain at the Great Lakes Center, an educator and a tireless advocate for restoring the environmental balance of the Great Lakes. Sadly, he'd died in his forties in a scuba diving accident in Lake Ontario doing salvage work.)

Our plan for the day was simple. Go out on Lake Erie, deploy a fishing line and catch lake sturgeon. Once hooked, we would bring her on deck, tag her, place an endoscope into her abdomen and assess the number of eggs and the overall health of the fish. It took a while to catch the first fish, but she was a beauty weighing 184 pounds. The females can live to be 150 years old and weigh up to 240 pounds. It's hard to describe how cool these fish appear in real life. Their bodies are elongated with armored plates. Near its mouth are tasting barbels that dangle like the thick whiskers of an enormous cat! The fish dates back to the Triassic Period and seeing one almost takes you back to the time of the dinosaurs.

We eventually released her back into the water, ventured toward the center of the lake, nearly to Canadian waters, and then deployed another line. This was almost a dream! I was out working with a group of scientists on a cool boat in an enormous lake, catching prehistoric fish, and monitoring the health of a lake that I wanted dearly to see recover from centuries of abuse. As we tried to catch our second fish, our line became snagged on something and we worked to haul it in. The fishing line was some ridiculously high test one, but it was clear that we had caught something much larger than a sturgeon. This had happened to me when I was a kid in Shreveport. You'd be trying to catch a bass and would hook a discarded tire instead. Eventually you would get whatever you had caught to the surface and be amused and/or horrified. Hopefully you would not break your line or lose the lure. We all watched that morning as the line was slowly worked in. Was it hooked on the bottom? Was it coming in at all? Then there it was. An elephant with flippers?

It is always hard trying to identify a sea creature from the deck of a small boat. I'd been whale watching a dozen times in Newfoundland—the bays south of the capital city of St. John's are teaming with humpback whales and seabirds in the early summer. The whales course back and forth, surfacing again and again, chasing the fish, and you see the occasional head, blowhole, dorsal fin and tail fluke. Maybe you see one of their side flippers here and there if they decide to roll. My point is that you need an active imagination to put together what an entire humpback looks like. When our "catch" broke the surface, all I could make out was a round gray wall which rolled to show a couple long slender flippers. There was a collective gasp from our crew. What had we brought up from the deep? Whatever it was, you could see that it was tangled in netting, likely discarded from a fishing operation.

Believe it or not, I had helped in the rescue of a large sea creature before when I was a grad student in Newfoundland. The sea life off the coast of Newfoundland is amazing. It was even better several centuries ago, before Europeans made it their mission to try to eat it all, but that is another story (told best by Farley Mowat in his *Sea of Slaughter*). The oceanography department at MUN had many disciplines. I was studying ocean physics, but of course, we

Atlantic Puffin
Fratercule artica

had people studying biology, chemistry, and geology, among other things. Early in my time in St. John's, I met a biology PhD student named Ralph Dixon. Ralph was toward the end of his degree and was more mature and experienced than me. He was married with a three-year-old son and living about 20 minutes north of St. John's in the fishing village of Flatrock. The coastline of Newfoundland is truly spectacular, and Flatrock featured a several-hundred-foot high sheer cliff right on the edge of the village, hence the name. Ralph was about the friendliest guy you could meet. He'd grown up in rural Nova Scotia and loved living in a community of brave and hard-working fishermen. The citizens of Flatrock all knew that Ralph was getting some fancy degree from the university, but they mainly knew him as the guy from the mainland who lived on the hill and liked to scuba dive. He had chosen to live in Flatrock because all he had to do was walk down to the fishing pier with his gear and jump in. He'd spend afternoons exploring the cove, untangling fishing gear that had been hung up on the bottom and stuffing unsuspecting lobster into traps. He was a popular guy when a fisherman would raise up a trap with six lobsters in it. That would never happen naturally.

So when a pothead whale ventured into Flatrock Bay and became entangled in fishing lines, his fisherman buddies wisely called their scuba-diving friend to come help. I was at school at the time. Ralph raced upstairs and stuck his head in the computer lab where he thought the majority of his fellow grad-students would be working on programs and research papers. "There's a pothead whale trapped in fishing gear up in Flatrock," he shouted. "I need some help." Young and stupid, we all went running down toward the department van and off we went. Most of us had seen pothead whales (or, more correctly, long-finned pilot whales) while out on research trips. They weren't as large and glamorous as humpbacks, but these were large, toothed whales comparable to killer whales in size. Their skin was dark, and they had this funny rounded skull almost like a beluga. I would later learn that they have the largest number of neocortical neurons (translation: the biggest brains) in the mammal kingdom. This makes them really smart, social whales, but they are prone to mass groundings. For some reason, this guy ventured into a fishing village and found himself all tangled up.

We stopped by Ralph's house to load up on scuba gear and wetsuits. As odd as this sounds, most Newfoundlanders can't swim. The ocean water there is just too cold for casual swimming, and most of the villages are too poor to have public pools. We found the whale just off the main pier surrounded by a half dozen lobster boats. These are working boats with large rear decks. One of Ralph's neighbors spotted us and quickly ferried us out to the whale. I have no idea how this creature got as entangled as he was. Ropes were wrapped around his whole body and trailing off in every direction. I should state the obvious at this point: Whales are mammals and need to surface regularly to breathe. We did not know how long this guy had been tangled up in these lines, but he looked exhausted. We had to act fast.

Ralph had a fair bit of experience with marine mammals from his time in college working at an aquarium. He stated that this guy was likely over 20 feet long and weighed over 4000 pounds. Getting into the water with him could be fatal. A desperate individual of any species can be dangerous. I once helped rescue a drowning man in a community pool. In his panic, the guy nearly drowned me and really scratched up my chest in the process of pulling him to the pool edge. To save this whale, we had to start cutting the ropes, but in order to do that, we'd have to be in the water. Ralph had decided that he was going in, but he was not going to wear his scuba gear. The extra equipment on this back would likely get entangled in the ropes and could lead to his drowning. I told him that I had some lifeguard training and was a strong swimmer. We both put on dry suits (you will freeze to death in Newfoundland waters in about 15 minutes even in the summer without a good suit) and snorkels. Ralph jumped in away from the long-finned pilot whale, moved in and started cutting rope. The fishermen had given us their sharpest knives. If you cut ropes for a living, you keep some sharp knives around. He cut through the rope like butter, but there were so many. I watched Ralph in awe as he drifted safely away, then quickly swam in to cut a rope tangled on the whale, and then backed off. He did this again and again. It was probably going to work, but it was taking too long. Ralph looked up at his friends leaning over the edge of the lobster boat as we praised his efforts and dexterity. "I can't get all of these by myself," he said. "Any of you stupid enough to join me?" He was looking at me. I had already psyched myself up to do this. I went to Newfoundland to have adventure on the water and experience its wildlife. I'd never get a better chance.

The water on my face reminded me how cold the North Atlantic is, but the suit kept my core remarkably warm. I worked adjacent to Ralph, giving him enough room but liking the idea that we were close enough to help each other if needed. He had started near the head on the "starboard" side, and we were working our way backwards. We were essentially shredding every section of rope we could get our hands on. As we made it past the pectoral and dorsal fins, the whale appeared to get a little wiggly. This was exciting and scary as he was now able to twist and flex. When he began to get some freedom, you could feel the power emanating from him. As he started to swim forward, Ralph and I kept cutting ropes and tried to swim forward with him. People on the boats sensed our success and started to cheer. When he swam forward, the ropes slipped away, and he was free. He swam near the surface for a few hundred yards and then disappeared.

Newfoundlanders like a party—and freeing a whale is as good a reason as any! Dark rum, Screech (a diluted drink soaked out of rum barrels) and beer all around to wash down all the fresh fish and lobster we could eat. All accompanied by frantic Newfoundlander music. (For those unfamiliar it has strong links to traditional Irish music.) The boys from the university were heroes, and the St. John's TV stations had a great feel-good story. Good times.

I wished Ralph Dixon was there with us as I stared at this giant lake creature tangled in what appeared to be a fishing net. I'd never given much thought to what commercial fishermen on Lake Erie used. In my time in Buffalo, I don't think I'd seen a commercial fishing boat. I knew a lot of sport fishermen and they were all using rods and reels. This was what appeared to be a gill or a pot net. Fishermen attach them to the lake bottom with weights and suspend them vertically with floats. For a gill or pot system, fish are supposed to swim into the net and get contained or caught up in them. Then the fishermen come by and collect the fish. The Great Lakes had an enormous lake trout fishery over a century ago. Millions of pounds of trout were collected annually until the sea lamprey, introduced by the legendary Erie Canal, resulted in the destruction of the trout population.

We all stood in shock on the side of the boat. What the hell was this thing? We were closest to its trunk, which was brown and appeared to be covered in glossy, smooth scales. I would estimate that its body was about twice the size of a cow. It was all wrapped in the netting and apparently unable to move its "arms." It had tried to dive a couple times since being pulled to the surface but now was too weak and appeared to be floating on its side. I could make out two slender flippers, one where its forelimb would be and one where its hindlimb would be. I presumed there was a matching pair of flippers on the other side. The flippers looked remarkably like a small version of a humpback whale's forelimb except that these did not have the amazing white color the whale's would have. This creature was much smaller than a humpback (thank God!) and its flippers were proportionately smaller, about three feet in length. As we were assessing the tangled mess of plastic netting around the flippers, the creature raised its head out of the water to breathe. We had gasped earlier when we saw the torso as it appeared at the surface, but we screamed when we saw the creature's long neck and head. It looked exactly like a brontosaurus, only much smaller.

My son, like most toddlers, had been obsessed with dinosaurs. Only a few years previously, we had spent hours together reading about and watching dinosaurs. Being a science and animal dork, I loved this period of parenthood and studied dinosaurs almost as intently as he did. Raptors, triceratops, stegosaurus—we learned them all. My favorites were the flying dinosaurs, but the swimming ones were cool, too. Was I looking at a living plesiosaur? Sixty-five million years ago, that would be the most logical explanation, but they had not existed in millions of years—or had they? While on vacation in Scotland about a decade before, I visited Loch Ness and learned about the theories to explain the monster. Other than a hoax, people have speculated that the creature was a seal, or a series of seals or a dinosaur. Plesiosaur fossils have been studied extensively. They were large aquatic reptiles with long necks, flippers for limbs and short tapered tails. They varied dramatically in size. My favorite was the enormous one, Elasmosaurus, which was as long as 40 feet and weighed up to two tons. There have been sea monster sightings in the Great Lakes since as long as there have been humans living along them. Nearly every First Nation tribe has stories of them. Samuel Champlain, the French explorer and founder of Quebec City along the Saint Lawrence River, claimed to have seen one in Lake Champlain in 1608. Sightings of the Lake Erie monster are so common that she had been given a name, Bessie.

But this was no monster. It was an animal caught in a trap discarded by humans. I felt a responsibility to make this right, just as my friends in grad school felt an obligation to save a whale accidentally snared in a fisherman's ropes. As the animal expert, I felt the crew looked to me for leadership. I pointed at the gear box and told them to get all the cutting items they could find. We set about cutting the fishing nets with the knives and wire cutters. There were five of us on board so we could move more quickly than my previous whale experience. This was a much different operation than the whale rescue I had participated in years before. First of all, none of us were going to jump in the water. Frankly, this creature scared the crap out of me. Early on in the rescue, he raised his head towards us. Fortunately, his neck lacked the flexibility to reach around and bite us on the boat. But when he opened his mouth, it was full of sharp teeth. I recalled from my dinosaur-studying days that plesiosaurs were thought to be carnivorous. Fortunately for our efforts, this guy was weak and not that big. Hanging off the side of the boat, we could almost reach all the way across his torso. As with the whale, we cut everything that was not flesh. I grabbed a flipper and Dennis leaned out and started cutting. This was both brave and foolish. One good swat could send me flying overboard, or worse, towards all those teeth! Just then, as luck or fate would have it, the creature stretched his neck back alongside the front of the boat and a couple of us started trimming the net away near his head. I called out to be really careful. In my years of vet practice, I'd been bitten numerous times, and would've hated to see the damage this mouth could inflict.

After about ten minutes of cutting lines, we were getting tired by this intense hand work but could see an end in sight. As with the whale, he seemed to sense when we were getting close to freeing him. Then all of a sudden, he came alive, thrashing his powerful flippers and tossing off the last of the netting. Suddenly, his head plunged under the water, his short and tapered tail appeared, and he disappeared in a froth of water. We started high fiving and hugging and congratulating ourselves when about 20 yards away he erupted from the surface like a breaching humpback whale. He generated much more velocity than I would have expected and came nearly completely out of the water, twisting around and then landing on his back with an amazing splash. What a paleontologist would give to see this! We presumed it was an expression of relief and the joy of freedom.

As we motored back to Buffalo, the conversation was frantic. Our group consisted of two biologists, a veterinarian, a fisher-man-turned-ship-captain, and his young assistant. The biology types immediately tagged him as a plesiosaur. We could not name the likely species, but it definitely was not large enough to be an Elasmosaurus. I interjected that sturgeon were prehistoric so why couldn't we have another prehistoric species in this lake. It was pointed out that the Great Lakes aren't actually prehistoric. They are rather young lakes, geologically speaking, that were formed by the retreat of the glaciers at the end of the ice age 10,000 years ago. The sturgeon had simply migrated in and flourished. You could see how a species of bottom dwelling fish could propagate for thou-sands of years but what about this guy? How many plesiosaurs could live in these lakes without being noticed? How long do dino-saurs live, anyway? We began to speculate on asexual replication. It's a fascinating topic. Dennis immediately played the cynic. This creature could not exist in this lake, he stated. We all laughed, including Dennis, as we reminded him that we had just seen it. But Dennis pointed out the difficulties in maintaining a breeding population in a closed body of water like this. We then noted the enormous size of the Great Lakes: Lakes Erie, Huron, Michigan and Superior are essentially one body of water connected by a couple large tributaries. Mother Nature always finds a way to survive. We pointed out that a number of reptiles—including boa constrictors, Komodo Dragons, and monitor lizards—can reproduce without a male by what is called parthenogenesis. A number of species of fish, including Nemo the clown fish, can change gender if necessary. Some fish can even reproduce asexually. If any dinosaur was going to survive the Cretaceous-Paleogene event (the one 65 million years ago thought to be initiated by the asteroid impact that led to the mass extinctions), it would likely be an aquatic creature like a plesiosaur.

Lake Erie's Bessie

We arrived back at the harbor, but did not make a pact to keep this quiet as my veterinary friends had with the sasquatch. No one was going to believe us anyway.

This would be a good time to explain why I have produced no photographic evidence of the cryptids I have encountered. Part of the explanation is that when these events unfolded (circa 2006), cell phone technology was evolving and I did not possess the smart phone I own today with its amazing videographic abilities. But more importantly, as first described in Chapter One, my colleagues and I had felt that recording these creatures could lead to their destruction. Please recall the violent circus that unfolded after the simple posting of the Clarence Sasquatch on my friends' farm.

CHAPTER FOUR

SOMEHOW I HAD KEPT RESCUING the chupacabra and the sasquatch to myself (with the exception of my friends at the Buffalo Zoo hospital and the stables). I had not even told my family, which was unlike me. We don't keep secrets from each other, but I must have thought that my wife would not believe me. Also, I didn't want her thinking that I was losing my mind, because as I drove home from the plesiosaur rescue, I really did think that I was losing my mind!

These experiences were a lot to process. Practicing veterinary medicine can be stressful as we deal with a lot of complex, and sometimes grave, matters. This can sound odd to most people, but veterinarians have one of the highest suicide rates of any profession. This is in direct contrast to the idyllic life depicted by the great James Herriott of *All Creatures Great and Small* fame. He made his years practicing in the Yorkshire countryside sound like a grand old time. And, most of the time, I suspect it was.

But even in his memoirs, Dr. Herriott's work was not always pleasant. My most emotionally demanding day at work occurred the morning after the passing of my favorite cat, Sarah. Even veterinarians have favorite pets, and she was an adorable, long-haired calico with the brightest eyes I've known. She had been my wife's cat from before we met, but Sarah took an immediate liking to me, and that cat and I would spend hours together petting and brushing and talking. (She was perhaps the most chatty cat I have ever met, and I've met a lot of cats.) Eventually she became ill with what I and my colleagues suspected was a cancer called lymphoma. We supported and doted on her for weeks until one evening I returned from my long day of caring for other people's cats to find her in distress. I took her directly to my friend's 24-hour emergency practice and we put her to sleep. This was especially hard for us because our toddler son had taken a liking to her as she often followed him around looking for spilled yogurt—her favorite food.

I returned home from the emergency clinic and grieved with my family and, in the morning, prepared to face the next day at work. My first appointment of the day was an emergency walk-in. The patient belonged to one of my favorite clients (vets have favorite clients too) and had been supported through several months of kidney failure, but she had taken a turn for the worse and had clearly reached her time for euthanasia. Trying to be the responsible professional, I began to review the options of checking bloodwork to see her status, or simply deciding to put her to sleep. It was at this moment that I could not contain my emotions any longer. I burst into tears and found myself unable to speak. The look on the client's face was a mixture of grief, concern and confusion. Fortunately, one of my veterinary technicians was in the exam room with us and was able to explain why her "other" family doctor just had an emotional meltdown. The three of us all ended up hugging and crying and comforting ourselves in knowing that our two cats had both had long lives filled with love. I cherish the fact that I get to help people every day at my job, and sometimes they help me too.

But we should return to the unfolding events of my life as I was not capable of internalizing these astounding developments any longer. I got home from my drive from the Great Lakes Center, opened a bottle of wine with my wife and told her all about these three crazy events. At first, of course, she thought I was kidding, and she did have good reason because I do like to make up stories and embellish them a bit. But it soon became clear to her that I could not make all this stuff up. She was excited and a little pissed off. Why did we not have her help us save the chupacabra? She was just in the room next door sleeping when we found it. How cool was it to see a real sasquatch? I had told her about finding one near my parents' house years ago, but she thought that I was making that up. Teenagers *do* have active imaginations, and my brother *is* a bit of a prankster. She'd never asked him to corroborate the story for some reason.

Now that I had told her about all these strange and wonderful and scary experiences, we both asked the same question—at the same time: What was I going to do? It seemed like supernatural forces were at work. My training and intuition had guided me through these experiences, but I was a little afraid of what waited ahead. I had been thinking about my old friend, Ralph Dixon, from the moment I saw Bessie, the plesiosaur. Our time rescuing the pothead whale was one of my fondest memories of Newfoundland, and we'd been really good friends during grad school. Stressful times can create lasting bonds. Grad school wasn't combat, but you do feel a special connection when you survive something together. Ralph and I had stayed in touch sporadically through email. He had worked as a post-doc at Dalhousie University in Nova Scotia, then was faculty at the Woods Hole Oceanographic Institute in Massachusetts. He had returned to Newfoundland to work at the Ocean Science Centre at Logy Bay just north of St. John's. My wife and I had seen Ralph just the year before the plesiosaur incident when he was at a conference in Toronto, which is pretty close to Buffalo. We'd spent most of the weekend with him, catching up on MUN and St. John's. My wife took a liking to Ralph, and she also sensed that he was the guy to call. So I did.

Ralph and I chatted for a while about family and work. His son had just finished his PhD in Environmental Science at the University of British Columbia, and that was amazing to both of us. He'd been such a funny little boy that I could not imagine him as a full-fledged scientist. To me, he remained that wild little boy who would jump off the couch on to his unsuspecting father while pretending to be a Mutant Ninja Turtle.

Ralph had moved back to Flatrock, and was living in a much nicer house than in grad school. A lot had changed in our lives, but he was still scuba diving and hanging out with the local fishermen. I can't explain how happy that made me. He started asking about me and my family and hobbies and work. After discussing my obsessions with endurance training and the fermentation of alcohol, I decided it was time to tell him my secret. I laid it all out for him. I told him everything—about the chupacabra, the sasquatch, and the lake monster. He was really interested. He took it seriously and asked a bunch of smart and probing questions. Then he shocked me with probably the most surprising thing any other person has ever told me. Ralph had been working the last year on a secret conservation program for mermaids (or "merfolk," more correctly, as there were mermen also). Upon returning to Newfoundland, he had started out working as an oceanographer for the Canadian government in the fisheries department. One position led to another and he ended up joining a group of researchers that sounded a lot like the X-Files-Meets-Jacques-Cousteau. The program was overseen by an arm of the United Nations called the International Union for Conservation of Nature and Natural Resources (IUCNNR). He wanted me to come to Newfoundland and work with him for a few months. It occurred to me as he spoke that he was really going out on a limb just by mentioning this project to me. The program had been considering the addition of a veterinarian, but you can't just place an ad for what they were doing. How could I say no?

I had to do a few things before I could make this trip happen. First, I had to temporarily get out of my responsibilities at my veterinary practice. This can be really difficult in a small practice, because veterinarians can be in short supply. Also, I love my patients and clients and would never leave them high and dry. Fortunately for me, we had recently hired a relief vet to cover maternity leave for one of my co-workers and now she was returning to work. Serendipity. The relief vet had enjoyed her time at our practice and was willing to stay on for a few more months. I have a good relationship with my boss, but doubted she would believe that I needed time off to go study merfolk. Such a statement could get you committed. So I told her that I needed to spend a few months working with some oceanographers from my past on some unfinished research. This was believable and kind of true.

Second, I needed a security clearance, and this was not your typical security clearance. One of my friends had joined military intelligence a few years ago and went through a security clearance. Lots of questions, but no big deal. For this clearance, however, I spent a couple days at a nondescript office building in suburban Toronto undergoing extensive physical exams, blood work, lie detector tests, psychiatric screenings and more. They searched my background and the backgrounds of just about everyone I knew. Truly a weird experience, but I passed. I spent the next week reading everything I could about mermaids. I knew that this was mostly a waste of time, but I figured what the heck. I even rented Disney's *The Little Mermaid* and *Splash* with Tom Hanks and Daryl Hannah. My adolescent son thought this was getting a little weird. Grown men don't spend all their free time studying mermaids.

The amount of literature and artwork on mermaids is astounding, and most of it was a waste of time from a scientific perspective, of course, but some of it was fascinating, and it wasn't just sexy women with fish tails sitting on rocks out in the ocean. There are so many eye-witness accounts, mostly dismissed as crazy or as false sightings of manatees, or sailors who had been at sea too long and were seeing topless women as part of some weird fantasy. Perhaps you've heard one of the many accounts of sailors near death adrift at sea being kept afloat by dolphins? Or mermaids?

From a scientific aspect, could merfolk really exist? Evolution can be rather weird. Look around. It's not hard to imagine a creature that evolved to live on land and then went back to living in the ocean. This describes the evolution of cetaceans (or whales). Thanks to recent DNA studies we now know with certainty that cetaceans are most closely related to the hippopotamus. The diversity created by evolutionary pressure is remarkable. A blue whale (weighing 150 tons), a hippopotamus, and a dolphin have a relatively recent common ancestor. Have you looked at a hippopotamus lately? How is that possible? But it is.

Merfolk appear in almost every culture's literature. The origin story of mermaids goes all the way back to the Greek myth of the goddess Atargatis who went to sea after the death of her mortal lover, a shepherd. My favorite mermaids appear in J.M. Barrie's *Peter Pan*. These are closest to the sirens of mythology, alluring creatures near the sea shore that draw you in with their songs and appeals but might drown you if you get too close. Of course, I took the opportunity to watch and read *Peter Pan* again. My brain was swimming with ideas. I had asked Ralph what I should do to prepare. He laughed and told me not to bother. You can't prepare for what we were going to do.

I flew into the airport at St. John's and was reminded as the landing approached that the flight path includes the Ocean Science Center and Logy Bay. The shoreline for most of Newfoundland is breathtaking, but the cliffs of Logy Bay may be the most impressive and beautiful. It was my first introduction to Newfoundland as a college student and seeing the natural beauty made me remember why I loved this place. Looking down on the Ocean Science Center on this isolated bay, on this peninsula, on this island, on the edge of the North American continent, with only one road in and nothing but cliffs and rough water surrounding it, it became clear to me that this was the perfect spot to conduct a top-secret study in mermaid conservation. Ralph met me at the airport, and it was immediately like old times. We went back to his house, and he showed me my room. I brought up the topic of merfolk when we were alone, and he quickly cut me off. We could never discuss the topic outside of the OSC. My excitement had caused me to momentarily forget the security agreement! We would start in the morning, but now it was time to relax. I was just another old friend visiting scientist.

We started early on a lovely summer day. The Avalon Peninsula has lovely summer days but not often. We spent the morning in briefings. I should have known that there would be committee meetings and paperwork. Down deep inside, well not so deep down, really, I just wanted to see some mermaids. I'm so immature. Eventually we got to the PowerPoint presentation by the head scientist Albert Gentry, who was a native Newfoundlander with a classic accent that made the presentation that much better. So many fond memories came rushing back.

Albert started with a clip of Ariel in Disney's *Little Mermaid*. *"Under the Sea, it's always better where it's wetter,"* so the crab sings. It turns out, however, that the quality of life under the sea had actually been deteriorating for decades, maybe even for more than a century. UN scientists had known about the presence of merfolk for decades, but had been keeping it under wraps for the obvious reason that it would freak everyone out. Before you say that it is ludicrous that a population of merfolk exists in our oceans, I would like to make a couple points. The oceans are huge, and we have only explored a fraction of them. New species are found in the sea (and on land for that matter) every day. Second, undiscovered populations of large animals exist on the Earth and have only been discovered by westerners recently. For example, in 2007 a population of 125,000 Lowland Gorillas was discovered in the remote forests of the Congo. If such a population of gorillas can exist under our noses in heavily-populated Africa, how much of a stretch is it to think that we have undiscovered species in the ocean? It's not a stretch at all.

Albert gave his "Known History of Merfolk" talk. He touched briefly on the mythology and moved into our current understanding of their population and distribution. They had likely numbered in the millions at the start of the twentieth century and had been distributed across the world's oceans. They were clearly mammals and appeared to be saltwater creatures. No freshwater species were known. The DNA studies on merfolk were incomplete so a common ancestor was uncertain. The photos and drawings of merfolk presented reminded me of primates. The torsos looked remarkably like a human's, just more muscular, and their arms looked remarkably human except for the webbing between their fingers. Their head, shoulder, and torso structure resembled that of humans, but below the waist it was a different story. From the hips down, they looked like dolphins, although they lacked a dorsal fin. In fact, the only fin they possessed was a tail fin. Like cetaceans, they were hairless. There was no flowing mane of hair so popular in art and mythology. Their eyes reminded me of seal eyes—large, dark, soulful, and glossy. Their lips were simple and their teeth were impressively sharp and pointy—clearly carnivores. Their ears were almost non-existent and their noses were flat against their faces with just a couple slits. Again, almost seal-like. Albert showed us videos of them swimming and it was almost hypnotic. Imagine the most graceful human you have ever seen in the water and then cross it with a dolphin. Powerful and smooth. It made me think of the seals at the Buffalo Zoo or the dolphins I'd seen.

As the video concluded, I met the scientists on the team—an impressive assortment of biologists, fisheries experts, geneticists, virologists, chemists, physicists, and more. What were we all here for? Al returned to the mission. Mermaids had been turning up sickened throughout the world. The IUNCCR had been managing this for years, keeping it quiet, but it was only getting worse. The prevailing theory was that people (or rather human overpopulation and uncontrolled consumption) had something to do with it. Were mermaids a bioindicator species?

We have long known that certain species are good indicators of the health of an ecosystem. The crudest example is the canary in the coalmine. Back before we had the scientific ability to monitor air quality in mines, miners really would take this fragile little bird down into the mines with them. If you were in a mine and the canary keeled over, you'd best get the hell out of the mine.

From a modern scientific standpoint, the classic bioindicator species are amphibians, frogs in particular. Amphibian populations across the world have been declining. Frogs have complicated life-cycles and are highly dependent on a clean environment. Changes in water clarity, temperature, pollution, depth, and more can have a profound effect on their survivability. If frogs are doing well, then environmental conditions are probably good. What does this have to do with merfolk? The team had been working on explaining the decline in their populations for years and felt that the research was on the verge of a breakthrough. Sadly, similar scenarios are currently being investigated in many species. Honey bees and right whales come to mind. The survival of both species has been stressed by the activities of people. In the case of bees, pesticides and habitat

destruction have pushed them to the brink with profound impli-
cations for our agriculture industry. For the Atlantic Right Whale,
after centuries of whaling reducing their numbers from the millions
down to the hundreds, their biggest threats are now collisions with
freighters when they enter ever-expanding shipping lanes or entanglement in fishing nets.

As a teenager, I became simultaneously aware of the beauty of
nature and of the callousness of the men in control of our world. I
wrote previously of my wonder at the wilderness I had experienced
in the woods of Louisiana and the deserts of west Texas. This was
the early 1980s during the rise of Ronald Reagan and his infamous
Interior Secretary James Watt. Together they launched a campaign
to open up as much federal land as possible to development. Oil
drilling, mining, and clear cutting in crucial habitats—these were
all fine with them. To paraphrase Watt, "When the last tree is cut
down, the lord will return." What sort of sick philosophy was this?
You certainly won't find that in the New Testament. I felt more
akin to John Muir, who wrote that, "Everybody needs beauty as
well as bread, places to play in and pray in, where nature may heal
and give strength to body and soul." This was the philosophy I was
searching for. It would lead me to oceanography, then to veterinary
medicine, and on to a deep respect for those who sought to care for
all creatures.

Shortly after entering vet school, I joined LSU's Raptor and
Wildlife Rehabilitation Unit. It was a club dedicated to caring
for injured wildlife. I threw myself into the club and soon found
myself caring for hawks, owls, kites, vultures, squirrels, sparrows,
pelicans, herons, opossums and eventually bald eagles. The medical
experience was excellent, but I grew philosophically, too. I travelled to conferences hosted by the National Wildlife Rehabilitators
Association. These were my people. The conference consisted of
veterinarians, technicians, biologists, and lay people who had dedicated their lives to caring for injured and orphaned wildlife. Bats,
birds, skinks, snakes—there was a rehabber for every one of them.
James Herriot would have been proud.

Some of my classmates made fun of me for spending so much of my potential studying time caring for creatures like a simple crow. Always up for philosophical discussion, I would engage them at whatever level I thought could persuade them. One of my Arkansas farm boy classmates had a fondness for Turkey Buzzards. You could tell from his tone that he had loved watching them soar over his family's property back home. I told him that my greatest honor would be to care for the California condors that our veterinary colleagues were working to save from extinction. Only about twenty of these majestic birds survived at that time (1997), and they were all being cared for by vets and rehabbers in captivity at zoos in Los Angeles and San Diego. I would tell him over a few beers to imagine the largest buzzard he'd ever seen and triple it. Condors in flight are often mistaken for small planes. For the fundamentalist Christian classmates (and we had a bunch of them at LSU), I appealed to the passages of the bible where God entrusted man with care for all of his creation. We were shepherds of the Earth, right? They must have thought I was weird, but I think they appreciated my honesty.

Atlantic Mermaid
Aquapithecus miravivens

So here I was in my beloved Newfoundland. In my element but entirely out of my element too. Surrounded by scientists who were experts in their field trying to understand an intelligent species that we could not communicate with. Al and Ralph took me down to the "aquarium" where the merfolk lived. There were six merfolk at the center at the moment. Four of them were adolescent. They were smaller and had not developed secondary sex characteristics. Ralph had taken to swimming with them and he wanted me to join them. This seemed weird but I guess we needed to meet them where they lived. The tanks at OSC were world class and they connected directly to the ocean. We slipped on some wetsuits and plunged in. That North Atlantic water was just as cold as I remembered it, but the wetsuit and the adrenaline would keep me warm for a while. The gates to the ocean opened and a surge swept us out into the bay. What a rush! Ralph had given me goggles so my vision was excellent. The merfolk came alive and raced out of sight only to return in a flash. They grabbed our hands and off we went. Such a blast! I felt like Michael when Peter Pan took him from his bedroom window and flew off to Neverland. My merman escort enjoyed it, too. He kept looking me in the eye and vocalizing high pitch sounds, similar to a dolphin's, that almost hurt my ears. After about ten minutes, we humans started to shudder and our merfolk companions/guides took us back to the tanks. They had installed hot showers along the deck for which I was grateful.

The humans returned to the conference rooms to review our objectives. Al started with the reproductive physiologists' analysis of the mermaids' estrogen and progesterone levels and sperm counts of the mermen. I presumed the obvious about how they had collected blood samples for the female hormone levels, but I really did not want to know the details of mermen semen collection. My mind kept returning to the sounds of the merfolk I had just met. They were trying to tell me something—I just knew it. I interrupted Al and the physiologists. "Can we communicate with them?" I asked. "That's limited. Mostly body language," was the reply. I related that I thought they were trying to tell me something. What they were saying, I had no idea. Everyone agreed that their "vocalization" had been noted many times before, but they took a doubtful posture at whether this was anything close to speech as we knew it, even though brain scans of merfolk songs had shown development in regions that neurologists thought related to speech. Trying to translate these "songs" had, thus far, proven impossible. Cetacean song experts had been consulted for years. Everyone has heard humpback whale calls before. Their eerie songs are legendary, but do they constitute a language? I was having flashbacks to

Jacques Cousteau's inspirational television shows. Human ability to empathize with cetaceans was limited by our terrestrial training. It had been a long day and I asked to return home (to Ralph's house) with the workbooks to do some catch up reading. Al, who gave the impression that he had real faith in me, gave me some recordings of mersong along with an underwater speaker. "Take a nice bath and listen to some Top 40 mermusic," he joked.

"I prefer Icelandic mermusic," chimed in Ralph.

At Ralph's, I read the binders for a while, then took a walk across the barrens and along the cliffs. With a cool wind blowing and the North Atlantic crashing against the rocks below, I decided a bath would be nice. Curious, I tried out the recordings with the fancy water speaker. There was something oddly familiar to these mersounds. I listened until the water started to get cold and I nearly dozed off—the jet lag was still pretty bad. Then it hit me. I had heard this before. My wife and I had spent our honeymoon in Hawaii on the island of Maui. While we did our share of relaxing, we explored the island as much as possible, and when in the car, we searched for Hawaiian radio stations and fell in love with the songs and the language. By chance, we met one of the celebrated Ho'opi'i Brothers while out for lunch. He was an interesting man and a phenomenal musician (as was his brother). We enjoyed his music so much that we bought a number of discs and continued to listen for years. Recalling that time, I was convinced that there was something Polynesian in these mersongs.

At the morning meeting, I told the research council my hunch. There was disbelief, but, as all good scientists do, they gave my intuition respect and were willing to test out my theory. As chance would have it yet again, my wife's best friend was a linguistics professor with a focus on Native American languages. She had bounced around after grad school in Buffalo and eventually ended up teaching in Hawaii. I suggested we contact her to see if there was any possibility that these mersounds had Polynesian origin. Some of the council were excited about this potential development, and some thought it was a waste of time. Regardless, St. John's was 7 hours ahead of Honolulu, so my friend was certainly asleep and we would have to wait. In the meantime, the security team would run a search on her, and our IT team would email her a demo recording with instructions on how to play it underwater. I was to call her at 3 p.m. Newfoundland time to ask her opinion on this "Beluga Whale" recording we had uncovered.

The meeting with the reproductive physiologists resumed. I appreciated that these bright people, all specialists in their fields, had welcomed me into their world. I was still unsure what I would provide, but I apparently had the respect of the leadership. We returned to the suspicions that the declining numbers of merfolk were the result of reduced fertility. The usual culprits for declining wildlife populations are many and include habitat loss, hunting, pollution, entanglement in nets, lack of food sources and invasive species. Sadly, we have recently added climate change to the equation. The ocean suffers from the increased presence of human-generated carbon dioxide in two ways. First, the ocean is simply warmer due to global warming. Second, increased atmospheric carbon has made its way into the ocean and changed the acidity of seawater. The effect has been named "global warming's evil twin" and has lowered the pH of the oceans from a pre-industrial level of 8.2 to the current level of 8.0. That does not sound like much, but when you consider that pH is an exponential calculation of the presence of hydrogen ions in seawater, the effects have already proven to be significant. Coral bleaching events in Australia's Great Barrier Reef and signs of damage to a wide range of shellfish are well known to scientists (even though certain corrupt politicians prefer to call this a "hoax" propagated by "the Chinese"). It was not a stretch to think that increased atmospheric CO_2 was contributing to reduced fertility in mermaids. We had no evidence that merfolk were being killed in fishing nets or that they appeared underweight due to lack of food. The reproductive specialists did have concerns about fertility, however. Sperm counts in the mermen were lower than those studied in other primates. They were also lower than known levels in whales.

Our next meetings were with maternal-fetal specialists. I was starting to love this new opportunity and wished that my father, the gynecologist, was still alive to share this. One of his heroes was

Kurt Benirschke. Dr. Benirschke started out his career as an MD pathologist at Dartmouth and Harvard Universities in the 1960s and moved west to help in the establishment of UC San Diego's medical school. His fascination with placentas and reproductive anatomy would lead him to collaborate with conservationists at the San Diego Zoo. He would dedicate his life to better understanding the reproduction of all species which eventually lead to the creation of cryopreservation of species, more commonly known as the "frozen zoo." My father met Dr. Benirschke during his work in obstetrics and gynecology and admired his brilliance and dedication. As I looked across the conference table, I could see that we were walking in the footsteps of giants and looked to them for inspiration. It was as we were reviewing ultrasounds of mermaid uteri that my twisted sense of humor speculated as to what you should call a merfemale once she was married when my linguist friend from Hawaii called.

I stepped out of the meeting to take the call. "You know that I'm not stupid!" were the first words from Ariel. (There was a certain irony that Dr. Eastman was named after Disney's version of Andersen's famous mermaid.) "That's not a whale song. It's some sort of Polynesian mash up. You are such a jerk. It's funny. Brilliant, in fact. Where did you find it?"

I was flabbergasted! My wacky theory might just be right. I started to almost hyperventilate. My mind was swimming with possibilities. These merfolk had been trying to communicate with humans for decades, just not the right humans. It all made sense. No people knew the oceans as well as the Polynesians. They had based their culture and survival on navigating the Pacific. As the offspring of Vikings, I was taught a profound respect for courage and seamanship in all forms, whether it's Roald Amundsen, Chinese explorer Zheng He, or Polynesian navigator Tupaia.

The merfolk and Polynesian seafarers had learned each other's languages eons ago, but how they learned them we may never know, although I presume that it was for economic reasons or some kind of inter-species cultural exchange. When I was in the water with my merman yesterday, he had been trying to tell me something in an almost extinct human language that his people still used. I took a deep breath and started to explain *The Whole Thing* again, this time to Ariel. I was getting pretty good at relating these preposterous stories by now. Ralph was listening in on the call and started chiming in to back up my explanation. The next day, thanks to a military cargo plane, Ariel was there. She started in on the strangest translation project in human history. I had struggled for years of my life to learn my limited Spanish. Within days, Ariel was having complete conversations with the merfolk via head phones and an underwater microphone in the sea tank. The merfolk were rather excited about this development.

They had known that their people were having problems with reproduction, but they lacked the medical expertise to do much about it. Their medicine resembled that of traditional Asia, our own First Nations, and other indigenous people around the world. Treatment was based on plants and remedies but lacked the scientific potential that had bloomed in human medicine in the last century. Now that we had our "Rosetta Stone" in the form of Ariel, our team of virologists, endocrinologists and other experts could begin the serious work of figuring out a solution.

My few months at OSC would pass quickly as we all worked long hours every day. Ralph and I spent most of our free time scuba diving. I had always loved spending time in and around the ocean, but my introduction to merfolk gave the ocean a whole meaning: It was magical now. I also started to study the Hawaiian language as intensely as my schedule would allow. At the same time, I was reconnecting with some of my friends from grad school who had remained in Newfoundland. They had always found me a little eccentric, but now I was constantly listening to Hawaiian folk music and doing my best to sing along. They thought I was just being quirky, but I had my reasons. Most of the OSC staff jumped into the mer tanks several times a day to try their best to speak with the merfolk. We did this for enjoyment but also to better understand their lives. Our IT team had been working with Canadian

Navy acoustics experts to create a mouthpiece that allowed people to vocalize underwater. With Ariel's instruction, I was becoming conversational in Mer. I have enjoyed my attempts to communicate with Spanish speakers on my travels in Texas, Mexico, and Puerto Rico. This was even better.

Days before I left, our crew became convinced that they had found the culprit. Environmental degradation had stressed the immune and reproductive systems of mermaids to the point where a typically latent herpes virus had started to inhibit the female reproductive cycle. I have long found the herpes virus to be fascinating. One of my favorite professors in vet school had dedicated his life to studying herpes. Humans are familiar with this annoying family of viruses as they cause cold sores, canker sores, mononucleosis, chicken pox, and genital sores. They rarely make anyone really sick or are fatal, and typically will go latent in your immune system only to flare up when you are stressed. Nearly all species of animals have their own herpes viral infection, and the housecats I treat in daily practice commonly show a variety of upper respiratory signs like sneezing and congestion when affected.

Vaccination has been shown to be effective in preventing the spread of herpes in cats and people. All children are vaccinated against chickenpox these days, and a similar vaccination against shingles is now common for older adults. In addition, nutritional supplementation with the amino acid lysine or antiviral pharmaceuticals like acyclovir and famcyclovir have been shown to inhibit the virus. After three fleeting months, I left Newfoundland knowing that there was hope for merfolk. Their partnership with human medical science was likely to improve their fertility enough to save the species. If only the root problem of human indifference and overconsumption could be corrected.

It was comforting to return to Buffalo, to my home, family, pets and regular life. My experiences with the mer had changed me. I recalled my time as a preceptor at the Gladys Porter Zoo in Brownsville. The Zoo hospital housed a Mountain Gorilla named Joe who had been ostracized from the Zoo's population of about ten gorillas. Joe had not fit in with the other gorillas for years and would cause all sorts of disturbances when returned to the group. I never witnessed this but cringed at the thought of the damage an upset Joe could do. Of course, Joe's forced separation was unfortunate as gorillas are social creatures. In the wild, Joe would have been driven out and been left to fend for himself. In captivity, he ended up living in isolation in the hospital with the keepers treating him as almost a pet and looking for a better habitat for him at another facility. Joe was gorgeous, three hundred plus pounds of muscle. I worked in the room adjacent to his pen, got to feed him every day, and we bonded to some degree. When I talk with humans about animals, I often talk about empathy and the ability to relate to another species. I've always felt that trying to better understand another living thing makes you a more complete person.

These mer had blown my mind. Right under our noses under the sea, a whole civilization of primates was living, growing food, hunting, making friendships, fighting off predators, raising merbabies. There was so much to learn.

CHAPTER FIVE

RALPH AND I STAYED IN touch on a daily basis for months via email. I was given a special secure email account and cell phone. It made me feel so important, like a spy or a diplomatic envoy. Mostly we used them to talk about the typical goofy things we were interested in, like where in Toronto you could buy that delicious dark rum they barrel-aged in Newfoundland. But eventually our conversations turned to fairies. My favorite story as a child was always *Peter Pan*. What kid doesn't love Pan? Its creator, J.M. Barrie, knew what we wanted: pirates, sailing ships, crocodiles, mermaids, flying, sword fighting, pranks, and fairies. In my heart, I had known that fairies were real. The scenes with Tinkerbell were always the best, whether she was tricking the Lost Boys to do her bidding or joining with her fellow fairies to raise an entire galleon from the sea and fly it back to London.

For my whole life, I found myself repeating "I do believe in fairies, I do." As a teenager out in the woods, I would see fireflies and imagine that they were fairies. As an adult, a belief in fairies has meant that I want to preserve a child's curiosity and open-mindedness. Recently, an adolescent boy told me that he did not believe in fairies. I explained to him with some seriousness that he should not make such statements as they can lead to the sudden death of fairies. Then he said it again. I became so frustrated that I had to walk away before risking injury to additional fairies.

But now I was being told by my very scholarly friend Ralph and his coworker, a scientist at the World Conservation Monitoring Centre, that they were actually collecting evidence that fairies live in Newfoundland and throughout the world. And oddly, or maybe not that oddly, the scientists were exploring a potential connection between fairies and mermaids. The calculating and the creative parts of my mind were swirling as I tried to wrap my head around this revelation. Chupacabras, Bigfoot, sea monsters and mermaids were all creatures that you could at least put your hands on. But fairies were real? Really?

Given my recent experiences, I felt obligated to believe that this needed to be treated seriously. Over the last few months, my scientific world had been turned upside down. It had been made clear that there was a world beyond what I had learned in orthodox texts. Mary Shelley's Dr. Frankenstein had explored a world outside conventional study. Hopefully my colleagues' exploration of this magical, natural world could lead to a more hopeful fate than that of Victor Frankenstein and his creature.

At the lab at the Ocean Science Center at Logy Bay, the efforts to better understand mermaid physiology and nutrition had been highly successful. The nutritionist had established that the merfolk are omnivores, meaning that they eat both plants and animals. There has always been a lot of variety of food types in the sea. As Americans, when we think of the ocean, we mainly think of traditional seafood, but merfolk have been cultivating the ocean's flora for thousands of years. While our ancestors were on land developing grains and plants that would lead to the foundation of human civilization, the merfolk were cultivating kelp and farming oysters.

The recently founded Merese linguistics department had made remarkable strides in the few months since I left Newfoundland, and had focused, along with a team of nutritionists from the World Health Organization, on better understanding the nutritional needs of the mer. This was an amazing opportunity for the advancement of the understanding of nutritional science. It had been years since I had seriously studied nutrition in vet school. It was never my favorite subject, but I appreciated how important nutrition is to the overall health of an individual and the whole species for that matter. The study of veterinary nutrition is overwhelming given the large number of animals we care for. It has taken scientists decades to reach our current understanding of nutritional requirements—essential amino acids, vitamins, micronutrients. Fortunately, the researchers at the OSC lab did not have to reinvent the wheel. They applied what we know about human and primate nutrition to the merfolk and, with the help of scuba divers and submarine crews, had been exploring "fields" that the mer had cultivated on the Grand Banks of Newfoundland. There is a wealth of plants that can be grown on the bottom of the sea and, for the most part, fish are really hard to catch when you have modest tools. Most merfolk do eat oysters and shellfish like lobsters, because they are easy to catch for someone with a primate's dexterity.

Ocean acidification had started to affect mer farming productivity. I have long been a member of numerous environmental groups and read about the concerns of scientists regarding declining biodiversity and how the changing climate would affect agriculture. Never did I think that climate change would have an effect on ocean plants cultivated by merfolk, but it makes sense.

Conversations with our linguists had revealed countless stories from mer history. Kelp had long been a staple of their diet, but kelp production had fallen off in the last century. There have even been famines in recent decades, something unheard of in their history. Human scientists had explained to them the concept of carbon production leading to global warming but such an abstract concept can be difficult for a people who have never driven a car or heated a home. The mer are familiar with boats and ships, however, and we were able to explain that modern fossil-fuel-powered craft were part of the problem. The mer did not care for these craft. They were loud, dangerous, and polluted the water though they did have a centuries-long respect for sailboats. I have noted their relationship with Polynesian culture. Apparently the mer have a long history of "catching rides" on the bow wakes of Polynesian vessels in the same manner that dolphin do. If you have never seen a dolphin riding the wake off the bow of a sailboat, it is hypnotic. I tried to imagine what it would be like to watch merfolk surfing such a wave.

Ralph had essentially become the cultural ambassador to the mer and had even been taken on tours of their civilization. His scuba diving skills meant that he was spending lots of time with them in the water, and the IT department had constructed mouth and ear pieces that allowed direct communication. I should note at this point that the well-being the Tom Hanks' character felt when in the water with Daryl Hannah was, sadly, not what our staff experienced. You need to be an experienced scuba diver to keep up with the mer. Ralph was, and he started picking up the mer language rather quickly and was regularly taken on underwater tours off the coast of the OSC.

The Grand Banks of Newfoundland are a geographical marvel. On most of the coast of North America, as you travel away from the shore, the continental shelf gets progressively deeper and deeper until you leave the shelf edge, and the depth then drops off quickly to about twelve thousand feet. The Grand Banks is the exception, with depths averaging 90 to 300 feet, and with these shallow regions extending offshore for over 500 miles. The combination of the cool Labrador Current coming down from the north and the warm Gulf Stream coming up from the south creates the most productive fishery the world has ever seen. When Europeans first arrived on the Banks, the cod were so thick that diaries describe catching them by simply throwing a bucket into the water.

With this in mind, it's no wonder that the mer were attracted to the region. Ralph was taken to their oyster beds, sea cucumber groves and kelp farms. The remarkable part was that to the casual observer these regions of sea might look like a typical bottom. Ralph was not certain whether the mer "camouflaged" their developments on purpose or whether their respect for the sea inspired them to fit in with the surrounding ocean floor.

Human activity has had a profound effect on the Grand Banks and consequently the mer. The commercial fishing industry has devastated the Grand Banks. Europeans have been exploiting it for centuries. Whales, cod, walrus, seals, auks, puffin—the list of species devastated by mankind goes on and on and on. All these species have been endangered, with some even driven to extinction by human greed. But the mer continued to live under the radar and out of sight. In the early 1990s, oil exploration started on the Banks with much controversy. The industry brought many high-paying jobs but at a huge cost to the ecosystem that had always been Newfoundland's life blood. With oil exploration came the eventual spills, and the linguists were now struggling with the mer to describe what this mysterious black liquid had done to their once pristine oceanscape.

Since the mer did not build cities per se, their most remarkable archeological artifacts are their cemeteries. The mer bury their dead in the sea floor then place symbolic stones on the grave sites— their equivalent of tombstones. Ralph learned that their skeletons break down quickly in the "soil" of the ocean floor which would explain why mer skeletons never wash up on beaches. Hans Christian Andersen wrote in "The Little Mermaid" that mermaids quickly turned to dust after death. Turns out that he was nearly correct.

As if learning these remarkable characteristics of merfolk was not enough, the Merologists (that's a real science now) have uncovered a relationship with fairies. For eons, these two civilizations have been living symbiotically. If you know anything about fairies, you know that they are fickle. Anecdotes abound of fairies that settle into homes and help people out with chores and such only to get mad at the other inhabitants and then create chaos. Fairies have even been blamed for a wide range of calamities. For example, recent history describes the sudden death of workers on a road construction crew who had cut down "fairy trees" earlier in the day. The people of the British Isles have long had a deep respect for fairies although that has fallen off as modernity has made people less connected with the natural world. Fairies can be helpful. Entire memoirs have been written by people who developed cooperative relationships with fairies who helped them run their farms and vineyards in an ecologically sensitive manner.

As I started discussing the fairies with Ralph, I recalled that the people of Newfoundland have a well-established relationship with fairies, but that it seemed to be based largely on fear.

During my time in grad school in St. John's, I spent as much time outdoors as my classwork would allow. I'm sure that my colleagues thought that I was a little nuts. Newfoundland is generally cold, overcast, rainy, and really windy, but this kid from Texas and Louisiana did not seem to care. Fortunately, my other supervising professor, Robert Grenfeld, had a similar love of the outdoors and had been raised in Liverpool, so he was used to lousy weather. Robert was a real character who loved literature, Guinness, playing darts, and arguing politics. And he had the best accent—working class Liverpudlian—which rivalled even the best Newfoundland accents, and that's saying something! At times I felt like I was talking to one of the Beatles. He became my mentor, and we bonded as friends almost immediately.

The first time we went on a hike together, we'd been working in the lab on a computer model for studying the wind-forced response in nearby Conception Bay. I'd put in a lot of time entering data and tinkering with the parameters, and, finally, we were making some progress. Science can be quite satisfying when your hard work starts coming together. Anyway, we were sitting in his office on the Memorial University campus on a sunny June afternoon celebrating our success.

"A beautiful day like this is too nice to waste inside," he said. "There is a lovely cove on this very same bay and it's only ten miles from town."

That's all I needed to hear. I actually enjoyed editing code and creating computer models, but what I loved most was exploring the Newfoundland countryside.

We picked up a six-pack of beer and off we went. After a twenty-minute drive, we arrived in the town of St. Phillips and went a little north along

Moose
Alces alces

the shore of Conception Bay to the trailhead. In the 1990s, there was almost no tourist industry in Newfoundland. In the decades since, the local chambers of commerce have figured out that you can make some serious money from visitors from the mainland and Europe, but they do expect some amenities. In this era, however, trails did not have signage, much less parking lots. Fortunately, Robert had been to this cove before and knew the way. We left the car along the side of the road and walked across a meadow toward a break in the woods. It was here that we saw the sign. "NOTICE: Carry bread in pockets when you are entering the woods." Robert had not noted this before. Bread? What for? Are the local authorities worried that we might get lost and starve? I have always tried to be a responsible hiker, so I generally bring water, a jacket, a knife, a compass, a lighter, and maybe a snack. Robert made a comment that our beer was a strong ale and that would be enough to sustain us. We went on to hike through the woods to an isolated beach known as Goat Cove and had a grand time watching seabirds, swimming, sunbathing, and drinking the pale ale. We also couldn't help but talk about nerdy things like grid spacing, damping parameters, hard drive space, and computing power.

Spending a couple hours enjoying the bay that I was trying to recreate with a computer was inspiring. It also led to a discussion of whether there was a *Contra*ception Bay and where it would be located. I would later learn that the first intact specimen of the Giant Squid was caught in Conception Bay in the 1870s. The Kraken, as the Giant Squid was called at the time, had been terrifying mariners for centuries. You must realize that sailors in the past would spend years in isolation on small ships in the middle of massive oceans. Being alone on deck in the middle of the ocean on a moonless night must have been scary at times, and people on night watch were known to disappear. Tales abounded of enormous tentacles reaching on to a ship's deck and pulling people to their deaths. Whalers commonly found such tentacles and squid beaks in the stomachs of the sperm whales they caught. Add to this the scars noted along the mouths of these whales and the legend of the man-eating Kraken was born. These creatures remained a mystery until one was accidentally caught by fishermen in Newfoundland in the 1870s. Ironically, the second one was caught the following year in Logy Bay, Newfoundland where the previously noted Ocean Science Center would we built a century later. The Kraken so captivated the imaginations of the nineteenth century that one would be featured by Jules Verne in his legendary *Twenty Thousand Leagues Under the Sea*. (The Kraken now adorns the bottle of a decent spiced rum and was also included in one of the recent Disney Pirate movies.) It was only when I returned home from the hike to Goat Cove and told my landlord Jim of our adventure that I learned that the odd sign about hiking with bread was attempting to warn us to respect the fairies.

Jim Long was an old time Newfoundlander. He'd grown up in St. John's—and was known as a Townie, as locals in this area are divided into two classes: Townies and Baymen (or Baywomen). St. John's is actually the oldest city in North America, founded by John Cabot (Giovanni Cabotto) in 1496. It has a remarkably sheltered harbour and has been a maritime hub for centuries. The city has a population of about 250,000 with universities, the provincial capital, theatres, museums, galleries and the like. It's undoubtedly the financial, political, and cultural center of the province. Once you leave St. John's, the island is populated mostly by fishermen, loggers, and working folk.

Jim was every bit a Townie. He'd been to the best private high school in St. John's and studied art and design at a college in Montreal. He returned to Newfoundland to care for his mother and worked in interior decorating and set design for the local CBC station. Jim never married or had children. After his mother passed away, he started to rent spare rooms in his house near the University. He only advertised for boarders at the medical school and grad school offices. He wanted to share his house with a more mature and focused student, not some rowdy undergrad.

It took a while for Jim to get used to my energetic and mischievous ways (I was only 21 when I moved in), but we would become close friends and remained such until he passed away in the early 2000s. Jim was an ideal person to know in St. John's. He knew darn near everyone and had traveled extensively throughout the province. He was also an antique collector which meant that he knew every hole in the wall shop at the many outports around the province. You wanted to get an authentic locally knit sweater for your mother? Jim knew the shop. Your friends were coming to visit and you wanted to take them whale watching? Jim grew up with the guy who owned the charter company. You wanted the best fish and chips? That's an easy one, only made difficult by the numerous choices. He was also the person to ask about Newfoundland fairies.

I never met Jim's mother. She passed away years before I moved to Newfoundland, but it sounds like she was what you would call a "mystic." The folklore of fairies (and pixies and sprites and nymphs and nature spirits) abounds with tales of people who have seen small people in isolated settings. Sometimes a few people witness the sighting of these magical creatures, but fairies would never appear at a public event like the Super Bowl. Fairies are known to be secretive and, generally, only visit open-minded people, especially children.

The most famous fairy visit of all time was to a pair of young girls in Cottingsley, England in the early 1900s. They told their disbelieving parents that they had fairy friends down at the brook behind their country house. The parents humored the children and asked them to take a picture of the fairies with their new fangled camera. The girls did just that and it caused quite a commotion. Their parents went down to the brook to look for themselves but couldn't find any fairies. The girls explained that the fairies only appeared to special people, and then, after the adults left, they took some more photos. These photos also included some gnomes. The events became a worldwide sensation and even caught the interest of Arthur Conan Doyle, the author of the Sherlock Holmes books. Doyle, at that time, was at the height of his fame, but was also mourning the recent and tragic loss of his child. As a result, he had taken an interest in all things supernatural in an effort to contact his son.

The people of Newfoundland are descended mostly from the British Isles, so it's no wonder that Newfoundlanders would have a relationship with fairies similar to their ancestors. In fact, the relationship is likely stronger given their less urban lifestyle. Jim's mother was apparently known throughout the province for her ability to convene with nature spirits. She must have been an interesting person. Her husband was killed in World War II, and she raised Jim by herself. She was not alone in having to endure such tragedy, as a disproportionate number of Newfoundland men were killed in each of the World Wars, which is typical of poorer communities (see *Battle of the Somme* for more information). According to Jim, she was an independent woman and very active. Apparently she went curling every Saturday night into her nineties! I love picturing a ninety-year-old woman tossing an enormous stone down a frozen sheet of ice.

Jim was uncertain about when her connection to fairies started, but he had been aware of it all his life. They had a lovely English-style garden at their home in St. John's—well-manicured grass, hedge rows, flower beds, rose bushes, benches, fountains. According to Jim, she spent a lot of her free time in the garden tending to her plants but also quietly talking, though she was discreet about it. A nosy neighbor would think she was simply talking to herself, but Jim knew that she was conversing with her fairy friends. The general lore for Newfoundland fairies makes them sound a little ominous—crossing a fairy could be bad for your health or your home. Jim had heard this many times regarding the local fairies but never from his mother. She would tell him that as long as you respected them and the fact that they were here first, you would have no problems. In fact, you and your garden might even prosper.

According to Jim's mother, the house was on a fairy path, and fairies would frequently congregate in the backyard for parties, because they love to sing and dance. You have likely heard of "fairy circles." This is a term used to describe circular spots in the woods where the grass has been found to be trampled down. These sites are thought to be the after effect of a fairy party. I was in disbelief as Jim explained this to me as we sat in that same garden. Then he got to explaining the part about the fairy path, which I will recount in my best version of Jim's voice. The man was a fantastic story teller (as are a lot of Newfoundlanders) and would get so excited about individual stories that his cheeks would turn bright red. At times, he would become short of breath and almost sputter. He would jump from topic to topic, get lost, tell a side story, and then return to the initial story more excited than ever. I could listen to him all day, and the man loved to talk. It's no wonder that he liked me so much. I should note at this point that the Newfoundland accent is quite distinct and really enjoyable to listen to. I suggest you watch old episodes of the CBC show *Cod Co.* to experience it (and also because it is *some* funny).

"Oh my son, the house was crazy in those days. I was just a boy but I knew that Mother was some special. You never knew when the fairy parties would start, but it was almost always after dark. I never had quite the gift that Mother did, but I could tell that something was going on in The Garden. Thinking back, I think that I was just reading my mother's feelings. She loved her fairies. Mother was honored to have them in her garden. But you could tell that she felt left out on those party nights. See, she was not allowed to participate in the parties. I asked what they were doing out there. 'Singin'and dancin'—fairy stuff, don't ya know!' would be her reply.

"Eventually, around midnight, the party would come to an end and this next part was what I remember like it was yesterday. Mother would walk to the back door as if she heard someone knocking, and she would open the door. Wide open, my son! Then Mother would open the front door. If I was awake, I would be told to. Most of these parties were in the summertime—thank heavens! But a few of them were in the winter. It did not matter the weather: rain, snow, wind—doors would be flung open and Mother would greet every fairy as they entered our home, as a proper lady would. And the fairies would walk straight through the house. You see, my son, our house was built on a fairy path. The fairies have been living in Newfoundland for ages. Yes boy, it's true. And you have to let them through or it can be ugly.'

"So don't cross a fairy. No way, buddy. You know that new coffee shop down on Duckworth Street? The one with the silly enormous cup hanging off the storefront. It won't last. It's on fairy land!'" I laughed, but he was serious.

"Don't laugh. You'd have to be a fool to build there. Mother always said that you should ask the fairies if it's okay to build, but you know darn well those fools didn't ask. Now before it was a coffee shop, it was a consignment store. Before that, it was a bakery. Before that, a dentist. I've been here for ages, my son. They need to tear down that whole building and make it a park. Call it Fairy Park." He was really pleased with himself. And he was right. The spot would make a lovely park with a fine view of the harbour and out through the historic Narrows into the North Atlantic. On a summer day, you might even spot an iceberg or two.

These revelations about his mother blew me away. I was living on a fairy path in a fairy town with the son of a fairy "whisperer." I did not sleep that night. My mind was swimming with thoughts of fairies (and not the sugar plum kind). I had been in St. John's for about six months at this point and had fallen in love with the city. It reminded me of a colder, more working-class version of San Francisco with its steep hills, the ocean, the row houses, the cloudy days. But St. John's suited me better. It was affordable, and just minutes from town there were icebergs, moose, caribou, seals, puffin, and whales. Before turning in to go to sleep that night, I asked Jim why we were never awoken by fairies. Sure, his mother had long passed away but we were still on a fairy path, right? Jim related that after she died, he would hear odd sounds at the back door some nights. He never actually heard the backyard fairy parties, but he would eventually awake to the fairies at his back door wanting to pass through the house—and it really freaked him out. So he called Father Duffy, and the priest came to the house and blessed it. I would later learn that this is common practice with Anglican and Catholic priests. The late-night knocking stopped. The fairies went somewhere else. I understood why he did it. The thought of fairies was a little scary. Without his mother as a liaison, you never knew what they might do. But I was so disappointed. I was really hoping to meet a fairy.

The next day at school I shared all of this with my friend Kurt and he listened with a straight face as I recounted all of Jim's crazy tales about his mother and the fairies and the fairy path and the blessing of the priest. Kurt worked in the Physics Department at MUN and was a bayman from the town of Carbonear on the far side of Conception Bay, "a metropolis by Newfoundland standards," Kurt had told me when we met. He had become a dear friend in the short time we had known each other. The guy was a scientist and a skeptic—but not about fairies. Living out in a small coastal town, fairy talk was just part of the normal conversation. I would learn later that fairies in Newfoundland culture were so common that collecting fairy lore was actually part of the University's folk-lore department's mission, and Kurt knew a lot about fairies. He actually knew people who had gone out berry picking in the woods with family and disappeared for days only to return thinking that they had only been gone for a few minutes. Living on Fairy Time? Or the people in outports that would swear that their new baby had been replaced with another child by the fairies. The baby (a change-ling) would look identical to their baby—but it would be different. They were certain of it.

These stories are endless, and some of them cross into the gruesome. At night, people would leave food or water out on the table in their kitchens for their family members who were lost at sea, and it would be gone in the morning. The fairies ate it. In other tales, people would awaken in the middle of the night to the sound of parties in the first floor of their homes only to find a sudden si-lence when they walked down the stairs. This would happen every night in some homes. To the Newfoundlanders, it seemed to me, the fairies where the equivalent of ghosts.

I asked Kurt about the bread and hiking with it for safety in the woods. Kurt was very much an agnostic and the bread comment really set him off. I had presumed that one carried bread while in the woods to provide sustenance in case you were abducted by fairies. Either the fairies were lousy cooks, or they just would not give you any food at all. My second theory was that maybe the bread could be given to the fairies as a gift. Kurt was pretty convinced that he had a better explanation. "It's that Body of Christ gibberish. Communion? The fairies are unholy. They stay away because you've got the bread. Maybe you could put some Holy Water in your Nalgene bottle, but bread's easier."

I did not know what to think of the comment that the fairies were evil. I did not like this. Kurt, like most Newfoundlanders, would often refer to the fairies as the "good people." I liked this much better, but the spookiness was still there. Across cultures, fairy lore has had a trend toward the ominous and other worldly. To some, fairies are spirits in limbo, souls that were not pure enough to make it to Heaven, but not evil enough to be sent to Hell. So they live on Earth indefinitely with us in the shadows.

The most wild explanation of all regarding the origin of fairies was that they had been angels in Lucifer's army. When Lucifer lost his battle with God for control of the Universe, the angels fell to earth as fairies. And, I kid you not, the ones who landed in the ocean became mermaids. This mermaid tie-in with fairies had always seemed a little far fetched until I started talking with Ralph about what the Merologists were learning.

Merfolk find fairies as mysterious as we do. They describe them in a similar other worldly way. It had been made clear from the anatomical, physiological, and genetic studies conducted so far that the mer are primates that evolved back into being sea creatures—a parallel evolution similar to the ancestral hippopotamus transforming into modern day cetaceans.

The origin and evolution of fairykind will likely never be understood. You just can't thoroughly study these guys. They don't complete surveys or leave DNA samples. And the current state of surveillance equipment does not pick up their activities. What the Merologists have to go on are oral histories similar to those of the Newfoundlanders—strange accounts of merfolk noting the presence and activity of elusive "spirits." The mer stories lack the ominous tone of the human ones since the mer do not appear to be as easily frightened as we are. Or maybe they were just better in touch with the natural world.

The best explanation comes from my friend Ariel. She and the OSC linguists had been working to record an oral history of the mer. I was fortunate to have been included on some of the earliest translations. They reminded me of the mythology I read when I studied American First Nations literature. I will close this chapter with her first draft of the mer's story of creation as it provides a feeling for how intertwined the mer of the Grand Banks are with the fairies of Newfoundland. The language is clunky as the translation from Mer to English is still being fine tuned, but it is worth sharing.

At first, there was no ocean, only sky. Then the rain came and it seemed like it would never stop. Many plants and creatures appeared on the land and in the sea. Eventually, sharks ruled over all the water world. Initially sharks had expressive eyes but eons of ruling and killing took the life out of them. Now they stare blankly, lifeless.

The molluscs appeared next. They were created to clean the ocean. The water was not always so salty. Later came the whales. There were not always so many types. The Orca came later to protect the "Banks" from the shark. Only the Orca could stand up to the shark. They brought a period of relative peace. The elders say the Orca created the Mer and we arrived along with the Kind Ones, *what people call fairies* (my emphasis). The Kind Ones looked out for the Mer. They taught us how to swim and what was good to eat and how to grow kelp.

We don't see the Kind Ones much anymore. Our fathers' fathers used to see them every day. Now we see them occasionally. They moved to land and only visit rarely. They come sometimes and "tease" us.

As I read this, I am drawn to reflect on Indigenous Peoples' relationship with the *coyote* (or more accurately, the *coyotl*, in the original Aztec). To them, the coyote was a trickster, but more importantly, he brought them fire, protected them from *evil moons* and created all the animals. Sometimes he was lecherous and a liar, but the people and the coyote seemed to have a timeless bond that connected them to the natural world. I presume that we will eventually learn what essence connected the mer with fairies. Maybe, with a little help, we could learn how to reconnect with the natural world around us too.

CHAPTER SIX

MY FAMILY'S CONVERSATIONS AROUND THE dinner table have always been a little strange. My father spent several years as a rural practitioner in Wisconsin and then moved on to obstetrics and gynecology in the army. He would often share the events of his day, whether he was removing some large tumor from a uterus or discussing sexually transmitted diseases. While serving as a public health doctor during the Korean War, he took a lot of pictures and would show them on some nights to his kids via our old slide projector. Some of the photos included the facility his team used to delouse soldiers, and others featured the local prostitutes that he "inspected." I recall once, when we were out for dinner, a disgusted diner nearby asked to be moved to a table away from this bizarre family. It probably did not help that my father had a loud voice and loved to laugh out loud. The weirder the story, the louder he became. My siblings and I generally enjoyed these stories and egged him on, asking leading questions.

It was at Thanksgiving dinner that I decided to share my new experiences in the field of cryptozoological medicine with all of my relatives. There wasn't much point in keeping this news from them any longer. My wife and brother were already well-acquainted with these tales, so I knew that they would back me up as to their truthfulness. I had wanted to start out by talking about my friends in Newfoundland and the mermaids and then lead into the fairies. Many of my family had visited me at one time or another while I was in grad school, and they knew what a beautiful and magical place it was, but my agreement with the

IUNCCR prevented me from discussing those matters. So, I went straight for the sasquatch tale.

As I related earlier, my brother and I had seen a sasquatch while in Louisiana and my wife and son knew Harold and Jessica, so I felt I had some support. As I told the tale, I was getting a lot of funny looks and laughs from those who were hearing all of this for the first time. It's a great story, but I could tell from their comments that they thought I was pulling their legs. When I reached the point in the story where we were treating Harry at the Buffalo Zoo, my mother blurted out, "Did Grampy ever tell you about the time he and that veterinarian from back in Westby saved a jackalope?" You could have heard a pin drop, then we all started laughing hysterically as if my mother had just pranked us all pretty good. But she was serious, and she started to relate the details. Why had we never heard this before?

When my father finished off his commitment with the U. S. Army and returned from Korea in 1955, he went into private general practice in Westby, Wisconsin. This was a predominantly Norwegian town in rural Wisconsin and medicine was a lot different then. The only other medical doctors in the area were his practice partner and the local veterinarian, Winston Frank. For four years, my father led the life of a country doctor. He treated children with mumps, delivered babies, cast the broken arms of farmers who fell off tractors, and raced around the countryside at all hours of the night, sometimes in blizzards. When I told my father upon returning from grad school that I wanted to become a veterinarian, he was really pleased and began to tell me of his fondness for Dr. Frank. "Best technical skills of anyone I have ever operated with," he told me. I found this statement to be a little odd because as a vet, I had no personal experience doing surgery with my MD colleagues, so I asked for clarification. My father switched into the tone that retired practitioners take when discussing the good old days.

In the 1950s, it was commonplace for rural medical doctors and veterinarians to help each other out with challenging cases. If my father's MD partner was unavailable, he would call the vet to assist with anesthesia on a case, or maybe he would "scrub in" and help with the actual surgery. Conversely, my father would find himself helping out with cases involving dogs, goats, pigs, cows, and horses. This would never happen in the present day as we have specific laws prohibiting this. My father developed a fondness and admiration for Dr. Frank, and they remained friends for years. When I said I wanted to become a veterinarian, he was thrilled and noted he had thought over the years that, in retrospect, veterinary medicine might have been a better career path for him. My family all knew of my dad's friendship with Dr. Frank. What they did not know was the jackalope story. My mother is what you could describe as a circuitous story teller so I will abbreviate her version of the story.

Western Jackalope
Parcevus antelope

After his time in Okinawa, my father worked at army medical centers at Fort Sam Houston in San Antonio and Fort Bliss in El Paso, Texas. While working as a gynecologist at William Beaumont Army Medical Center in El Paso, my father would often travel to smaller neighboring army hospitals as an educator. The larger army medical centers are teaching hospitals, and gradually my father was becoming as much a teacher as a doctor. Dr. Frank had served in World War II and had stayed in the army reserves. My father and he arranged to meet up at an educational seminar at Fort Huachuca in the southern Arizona desert.

As my mother started to relate the jackalope tale, it dawned on her that my father had written about it in his journal. He had started keeping one while a soldier in Korea and often kept notes when he traveled or did something that he found interesting. She ran off to the study and returned with his journal—a tattered old leather book given to him by his Uncle Pearl, of all people. She handed the journal to me and commented that the jackalope incident had happened about a year after we moved to El Paso, likely 1977. I would have been about ten years old back then. I started flipping through the pages, looking for references to Dr. Frank or Fort Huachuca or jackalopes. There was a ton of interesting stuff in here that I could not wait to read at a later date. Eventually I found what we were all longing to hear. So I read it out loud to the table.

April 12, 1977—Fort Huachuca, AZ
Arrived late to base, about 10 p.m. Missed out on having dinner with W ("W" was how my dad referred to Dr. Frank). Drive from EP longer than expected. Still not used to driving in the desert. The roads are so flat and straight, hard not to speed. Sunset over mountains amazing. Have seen more colorful sunsets since arriving in EP than have seen in the rest of my life. Nearly hit a coyote. Damn near drove off road swerving to miss it. Got to get some rest, rounds at 6 a.m. and then zoonotic conference through the day.

April 13, 1977—FH, AZ
Strangest damn day of my life. Thank heavens for Dr. Frank!! Morning rounds and conference were routine. Great to see old friends. Meeting wrapped up by 2:30 p.m. so drove Winston to nearby Coronado Monument to hike near Miller Peak (9400 ft elevation) on the Mexican border. No one on the trail in remote AZ on a Tuesday. About 1 mile from trailhead, we found what appeared to be two dead jackrabbits entangled in what I first thought was a tumbleweed. As we approached, noted that the tangle at their heads was not a tumbleweed. Both rabbits had small antlers that had interlocked and were actually alive but exhausted and likely playing dead. One of the rabbits was badly

cut across the top of his head and neck. W stepped in to grab each of the rabbits by the base of their antlers and slowly and gently worked to pull them apart. Once free, the uninjured rabbit exploded off across the desert. Man was that bunny fast! W wrapped up the injured one in a light jacket (we did not actually need it on this warm day) and we walked quickly back to the car. The conversation on the way back to the base ranged from the medical aspects of what we would need to fix up the rabbit (the base had a small vet hospital so we should be ok), to did we really see two jackalopes? I had always thought these creatures were just a taxidermy trick— stuff a jackrabbit and attach the smallest deer antlers you can find. Once at the gate, W drove straight to the base hospital. The MPs escorted us in when they saw we were Lt. Colonels and told them we had an injured rabbit. Must have been animal lovers. W had me hold an anesthesia mask on his face while he shaved and cleaned the wounds—just like old times. The wounds could have been worse, mostly punctures from the antler tips. W thought this little guy was more exhausted than anything else. We sutured up the five or six punctures and placed him in a moderate-sized dog kennel. We used dissolvable suture for the wounds so that they would eventually fall out. We covered the kennel with a dark sheet and went back to the base hotel.

April 14, FH, AZ—7am
Just returned from rabbit release. I really should be better about bringing a camera on trips. No one is going to believe this one. W and I were up at 5 a.m. Took the rabbit back out to location where found yesterday. Opened carrier and he ran off into desert. Apparently he was mostly unharmed. W had fed him carrots, lettuce and apples through the night last night to rehydrate

him. Smart move! We decided that we would keep this to ourselves. Don't want to jeopardize our careers with a Section 8 violation. Made plans to visit Westby in January for ski jumping competition.

7 p.m.

It was really hard to concentrate at meetings today. Kept thinking of that crazy rabbit. Got to get to bed early for drive home tomorrow. Plan to stop at every crummy gift shop on way home looking to buy a stuffed jackalope.

As you might expect, there were a lot of attempts from my family to interrupt the reading, but I managed to cut them off and contain the wise-cracking to a minimum. First to speak was my cousin Mike, who had always been close to my father. "Crazy old fart is pranking us from the grave," he cracked. This got a lot of laughs, as you might expect.

"I believe him," I said. "I've seen some weird stuff this past last year. The sasquatch is only part of it." The consensus at the table was that both my father and I were delusional. "The apple doesn't fall far from the tree," was said more than once that night. Given my recent renewed interest in cryptozoology and my knowledge of veterinary medicine, I started to engage the skeptics. Jackalopes have been part of folklore for centuries. The first accounts of them are from Europe in the sixteenth century. A lot of creatures grow antlers. They are a characteristic of the deer family, *cervids*. Male deer, elk, moose, reindeer, and caribou all have them. The antlers are an extension of the skull. They start from a pedicle and form as a rapidly growing bone. Once they reach full size, the soft outer velvet falls off and the bone dies and hardens. But the antlers remain and are used for fighting and to impress the ladies of the species.

What's to keep a rabbit from having this odd mutation and grow a set of antlers? And this antler entanglement was entirely plausible. Many species of animals use their horns and antlers in fighting. You have undoubtedly seen male sheep dive headlong into one another in nature documentaries. They do this to demonstrate dominance and establish themselves as the best male for breeding. Antler entanglement happens all the time. It's not unusual for people to find a pair of dead bucks out in the woods with their antlers joined together. Why wouldn't a rabbit with antlers do the same? Male rabbits are actually aggressive with each other. If you have two male rabbits in a hutch, you have to be careful as they can really hurt each other. We think of bunnies being timid little creatures, and they are when it comes to interacting with people or predators. But with each other, that is not the case.

I made my best case with the family to explain that what we had just heard was possible. Why would my father lie in his personal journal? The kinship that I felt with my father and this veterinarian from another generation was substantial. I returned to my tale about the sasquatch from Buffalo, but I think that many of them had heard enough cryptozoology by now. The meal was mostly over, and people wanted to spread out a little as often happens at large family gatherings. I gave it another try with my story about Bessie, the Lake Erie monster. I told the abbreviated version, and my nephew loved this one. He had just joined the Navy and wanted to hear anything about the ocean (or a large lake, in this case). We went off to talk with my brother and another cousin, DG.

DG loved hearing my dad's story about the jackalope. He had always been close with my father and idolized him while growing up. He and my dad had a lot in common. DG also joined the army, and would eventually go to medical school. He was so excited about finding the journal and was looking forward to getting his hands on it too. As I sat with them in the kitchen drinking after-dinner cocktails, I started to reminisce about a story DG had told me when I was a teenager. I never did believe this tale, but recent events had definitely made me reconsider. The summer I graduated from high school, my father and I drove up to Wisconsin to meet up with my cousins and their father, my uncle, Don. The next day we would drive into Ontario to north of Lake Nipigon and then fly farther north on a float plane for a week of fishing. We were in the middle of nowhere, and the fishing was amazing.

The five of us would spend the day out in small boats catching as many Walleye and Northern Pike as physically possible. When you are out in cabins in the woods for a week, there is a lot of down time that leads to joking around and storytelling. One night after everyone had retired to their cab-

Walleye
Sander vitreus

ins, DG and I were hanging out. Despite being a physician and a Lieutenant in the army (at the time), my cousin remained remarkably immature (which I kind of admired). For example, days before on the drive north to the float plane, he entered the single stall bathroom at a rural gas station. There were a number of us behind him in line waiting for the toilet and he knew it. So DG proceeded to make every fart sound he could for his audience waiting outside. It was impressive. He was remarkably loud and demonstrated a wider range of sounds than I had ever heard anyone make before. As he exited with a huge smile on his face, he made some comment about feeling much better. So you can see why I was a little suspicious when my cousin started telling me about things I should be afraid of in the deep woods that night.

My older brother had warned me to beware of my cousin's tricks. DG is about six years older than my brother Brad and had ruthlessly pranked his younger cousin throughout their youth. I should also note for reference that this fishing trip to the Ontario woods had occurred about one month before my brother and I discovered the sasquatch behind our house. I was by this time an amateur naturalist, capable of fishing, canoeing, swimming in murky Louisiana lakes, and able to navigate unfamiliar woods as well as just about anyone. I was not, however, comfortable being in a strange place several hundred miles from the nearest town. I sensed that my cousin knew this as he launched into his best scary stories. He started by talking about the Algonquin Rattlesnake but gave up on that line when I started sharing tales about the alligators in my backyard pond in Shreveport and the rattlesnake that my mom and her zookeeper friends had trapped inside our house in El Paso. He switched to stories about the wolf packs that roamed the north woods and that led me to discuss Farley Mowat's *Never Cry Wolf,* which I had just finished reading. It had just been turned into a movie and chronicles a researcher sent to study wolves in the Canadian Arctic and the bonding experiences he has with the pack. I related to my cousin that, other than seeing the Northern Lights, hearing—or better yet seeing—wolves would be the highlight of my trip, and of my whole young life for that matter. In retrospect, I think DG was becoming a little frustrated with his attempts to cause his young cousin to have nightmares and decided to kick it up a little bit.

As I write this now, after everything I had experienced in the last six months, the irony of this tale is astounding. What follows is a modified account of what DG told me that night. My cousins had been to this fishing camp a number of times since adolescence. The most recent trip was a few years before when they came up with their dad and several friends from high school and college. It had been much like the many trips before except that time it likely included more beer and scotch. The fishing was great as always, and they started exploring the nooks and crannies of the lake's shoreline. The best Northern Pike fishing was located directly across the lake from the camp in a region that transitioned into a marsh. Fishing that location was almost like a study in fish communication. If you have ever fished for Northern Pike, you know that they are an aggressive fish and attracting them is typically not subtle. You toss out a shiny lure with a high test line, reel it in and repeat. Once you catch a little pike, the message appears to go out to the other pike that there is action, and you progressively catch larger and larger pike. Eventually, at this lake, you start catching some seriously big and toothy fish. They are actually a little scary to handle.

After a while, DG and his friend Bill decided to paddle along the shore and try to figure out if a stream was creating this marshy area that was a mecca for pike. Both of them were Eagle Scouts, so they knew they should do their exploring in pairs. They set off on foot and skirted the wettest region.

Beaver
Castor canadensis

Eventually they found the stream that fed the marsh. At this latitude, the vegetation is rather sparse so walking in the woods is easy. Growth rates are slow and a ten-foot tree could be hundreds of years old. They wandered on along the stream and up in the distance saw a large beaver dam with what appeared to be the world's largest and hairiest beaver lying along the top of the den. As they approached, they realized that this was not a beaver, but actually a large primate that had fallen partially into the beaver dam and had become stuck between the logs making up the dam. This was not the first dam these scouts had seen. DG recalled for his friend that many parts of North America were inhabited by enormous beavers up until the recent Ice Age. People like to talk about Woolly Mammoths and Sabre-toothed Tigers, but can you imagine a several hundred pound beaver? What kind of damage could one of those do to a grove of trees?

As they approached the dam slowly, they knew this was not a prehistoric beaver but possibly a bear. But its coat was not dark enough to be a Black Bear, and Ontario does not have grizzlies. As they neared the dam, the creature twisted over to look at them, and they quickly recognized that this was what he called a yeti. (It should be noted at this point that my cousin misuses this term to identify a sasquatch. The yeti is a large hairy primate of the Himalayas known to westerners as the Abominable Snowman.

Numerous cultures across the world have noted large human-like species living on the fringes of society. They are so common that they have been given their own genus, *Gigantopithecus*.) This face-to-face recognition scared all parties. DG and Bill started running back toward the canoe. As they rounded a curve in the stream, DG looked over his shoulder to see how close behind them this creature was. It hadn't moved. He stopped running and called to Bill to hold up. It occurred to him that the yeti might be struck in the dam. Against their better judgement, they returned to the dam to check out the situation. As they approached, it became pretty clear what had happened. The yeti had been walking across the top of the lodge, and his massive weight caused it to collapse entrapping his leg. My fearless cousin suggested that they start pulling away the logs to free him. His dumbfounded friend suggested they run like hell back to the camp and call for the float plane back to civilization. DG ignored his friend and started to work pulling out sticks and logs outside the reach of the beast. Yeti are quiet and secretive creatures and do not like having a person just out of arm's reach. As my cousin approached the lodge, the creature let out some pretty terrible screams. Maybe you have heard reproductions of these sounds on a cable channel's sasquatch hunting program. Bill just about wet his pants every time the yeti screamed. The beast also beat on the beaver dam a few times initially which nearly shook DG off into the water. Eventually the yeti appeared to realize that DG was not there to hurt him.

Dismantling a beaver dam is a major task. These aquatic rodents know how to build a sturdy home. Fortunately the yeti had done major damage to the lodge when he fell through, and as DG sized up the logs, he saw a way to get him out. The yeti's leg was pinned between a couple of the longer logs. My cousin suspected that from the yeti's close proximity that he could not get any leverage on these particular logs. DG started to twist and rotate a certain log farther away from the yeti, and slowly it started to move. This really agitated the creature as he did not like that this stranger was twisting the object that had his leg pinned. As the log started to move, it was likely rubbing unpleasantly along his sore leg. But as it moved, the once trapped yeti started to pull at the log and assist. Eventually, his leg was free and he jumped onto the lodge and started hobbling off into the woods never to be seen again.

As I sat in the kitchen with my brother and cousin, my nephew summed it up well: "What is it with you guys and Bigfoot? I'm never going camping with any of you ever again."

CHAPTER SEVEN

U PON RETURNING HOME FROM OUR family visit for Thanksgiving, I found myself reminiscing about my adolescence growing up in the high deserts of El Paso and southern New Mexico. My mother lent me my father's journal where he chronicled the jackalope rescue, and I immersed myself in it, looking for hints as to why my life had taken this strange turn.

Reading your parent's journal is generally fascinating, something to connect you to your place in humanity. As I said before, my father had an interesting life, and the journal made me long to see him again. His passing was not that long ago, and it was therapeutic to learn his thoughts unfiltered. He restarted his journal after we moved to San Antonio, and a lot of it was about his development as a doctor and an officer in the army. Much of it was about his hobbies and his relationships with his kids. My dad was a huge sports fan and wrote at length about his joy when the San Antonio Spurs won the NBA championship in 1999, 2003, 2005 and 2007. I'm a huge Spurs fan too, and we would talk on the phone almost daily during the playoff runs. His journal entries were almost comical with the detail they contained regarding player performance, coaching decisions and officiating. It was almost as if he considered himself an advisor to the team.

To my surprise, the pages contained a lot of comments about difficult career and medical decisions he had made over the years. He'd reached the rank of full colonel and been deputy commander of a large army medical center in El Paso, and was later acting dean of the medical school in Shreveport. To me, he'd always seemed so certain in his decisions, but apparently he'd agonized in private. I have always felt that uncertainty was one of my greatest faults, but my dad radiated confidence. He often joked with me and my siblings: "Never in doubt, often wrong." This comment was generally reserved for his medical colleagues who came across as overly sure of themselves. Reading my dad's journal made me feel a little better about my own bouts of uncertainty.

The journal reminded me of the day our neighbor's three-year-old son nearly drowned in their backyard pool. We were in our own backyard when we heard cries for help from the yard just below us on the hill. Lying on the deck next to the neighbor's pool was a lifeless kid with his screaming mother beside him. My sister went to call for an ambulance, and my father rushed over to their backyard. El Paso is really hot in the summer, and a lot of houses have pools. I knew that the little boy had been learning how to swim under the supervision of his mother, but apparently something happened that morning and he was temporarily unmonitored and either fell into the deep end or became over-confident and ventured out above his head.

Regardless, I watched in horror and anticipation from our yard overlooking theirs as my father sprang into action. I was about twelve at the time, so I didn't really understand how CPR worked. All I could process was that he was quickly moving back and forth from the kid's chest to his face for what seemed like an eternity. Several neighbors were standing around petrified by the scene when all of a sudden the kid started moving and the small gathering erupted in joy and tears.

Most of us spend our adolescence thinking that our parents are pretty special—whether they really are or aren't. They are smarter than us, taller, wiser, more worldly, richer, stronger. We idolize them. I'd just seen my father calmly step in and bring someone back from the dead, and my estimation of him went through the roof. He wrote about the incident in his journal in his usual casual way. Of course, at this point in his life he'd been a surgeon, a combat doctor in Korea, and was currently chair of the Department of Obstetrics and Gynecology at an army medical center. Stressful situations and saving people's lives had become routine to him, but it wasn't routine to twelve-year-old me watching him save a kid's life, and, reading between the lines of his account, I could feel his satisfaction in saving this little boy and what it meant to their family.

As I scoured the journal looking for more information on jackalopes or any other cryptids, I was sadly disappointed. There was lots of fun stuff but nothing relevant to my current metaphysical dilemma. I made copies of the journal and sent them to my brother and cousins hoping they would find some hint that I missed. But they found nothing of cryptid interest either.

Common Raven
Corvus corax

I could not stop thinking about the mountains of west Texas and southern New Mexico and jackalopes started to enter my dreams. Images of our pet rabbit, Felix (full name, Mr. Felix B. Rabbit) with antlers began to fill my subconscious. My imagination was getting the better of me.

My parents, siblings, and I had spent a lot of time in New Mexico as a family—skiing, hiking, and fishing. I called my friend and college roommate, Dave, who had gone on to become a psychiatrist. It is always good to catch up with old friends, but in this case it was more like therapy. Given my confidentiality agreement after my time at the mermaid institute, I had to be careful what I disclosed and decided to limit the conversation to learning that my father claimed to have rescued a jackalope in the Arizona desert and that I could not stop thinking about it. Dave did not believe the jackalope story and suggested it was likely a joke. But I knew that Dave missed my Dad, too, as he had been a mentor to him while studying in medical school. He suggested that I needed a vacation and that we should take a trip to New Mexico to clear my overstimulated and grieving mind.

My family had moved to El Paso in the summer of 1976, when I was eight years old, and my parents embraced the desert. Military families have a saying: "Bloom where you are planted." When you join the service, you'd better be prepared to be relocated and probably relocated again and maybe again. We had loved living on Fort Sam Houston in San Antonio. Central Texas is a unique and lovely part of the country with rolling hills, lakes, streams and a wide range of interesting trees and wildlife. Our transplantation to the desert of El Paso had made my family miss lush, sub-tropical San Antonio, but my parents were determined to enjoy west Texas also. That meant lots of trips to Cuidad Juarez across the Rio Grande to check out a new culture, the restaurants, race track, and markets, and eventually we traveled north into New Mexico to explore the southern Rockies.

Having grown up in Wisconsin, my father missed playing around in the snow. My mother, on the other hand, was happy to have left cold weather behind (and would never move back). When my father learned that the Sacramento Mountains near Ruidoso and Cloudcroft, New Mexico were tall enough to have ski resorts (Sierra Blanca is over 12,000 feet in elevation), he was determined to check them out. They were a two-to-three-hour drive from El Paso which meant an easy weekend trip or even a day trip.

We soon became a family of skiers, at least my father, brother, and me. It's odd what you remember most clearly from childhood. To this day, I can picture my father driving on those icy mountain roads with a car full of kids. We'd all be tired and happy following a day on the slopes, and Dad, who had spent years driving on frozen Midwestern roads and was confident in his winter driving skills, would tease us by pretending that he'd lost control of the car and we were all about to plunge off the roadway and fall thousands of feet to our deaths. I thought this was hilarious, but my teenage sisters would scream from the backseat of our station wagon: "That's not funny!" My brother would agree in a more sober and serious voice that "It's not that funny." And my Dad and I would howl as he managed to navigate the turn and we would all live to tell the tale. Later in life I tried this prank on my wife on our honeymoon on a treacherous drive along the cliffs in Maui called the "Road to Hana." It didn't go over well with her—at all—and I did not try it twice.

My parents would grow to love Ruidoso so much that they would buy a second home there that they maintained until well after we moved to Louisiana. As I reminisced with Dave about the college trips we made together to my family's house over spring break or in the summer, it became clear that something was drawing me back. It was an easy sell to my wife and son to travel to Ruidoso for some outdoor fun. We were going to be a little late to do any skiing, but the mountains have something to offer in any season. We had been to visit my sister in Lake Tahoe the previous summer, and this would hopefully be a repeat of that enjoyable vacation. My wife knew how much I had loved living there and rightly presumed this trip might act as therapy following the loss of my father. She had heard many stories of our adventures in the mountains and that I had learned to fish with my father in the streams around Ruidoso. The New Mexico Fish and Wildlife Department had a trout hatchery there, so the streams were typically loaded with rainbow and other species of trout. We would walk the streams for hours trying to hook a fish, listening to the water and birds. My parents had always been intent on catching dinner, but I just wanted to be out exploring. There was no fishing in El Paso *because there is no water* other than the Rio Grande, and I doubt that the fishing is worthwhile there.

We decided to stay at the Thunderbird Lodge in "downtown" Ruidoso. Given my renewed interest in cryptozoology, I started reading about the mythical creatures of the southwest and was pleasantly surprised to learn that it was dominated by creatures from Indigenous stories. I read about them as though I was preparing for a test and, if past experience was an indicator, I just might be tested.

As I noted previously, Indigenous Peoples have a different relationship with animals than settlers from Europe. Creatures like the coyote and bear are often written about like they are relatives or ancestors. I've always loved seeing wild coyotes as they look like the craftiest dog ever. You can see why they were described as tricksters. Bears, however, have always freaked me out. As an outdoorsman, I have read about bear safety in the woods my whole life. Carrying pepper spray. Wearing bells on your shoe laces. Keeping coffee cans filled with marbles. Hanging food from trees in a "bear bag" when camping overnight. I've spent my life trying to rationally conquer my fears but have come to suspect that I have a genuine bear phobia (kind of like Stephen Colbert).

The reality was that I came by my fear of bears honestly and it started one day in New Mexico. Dave and I had driven from Shreveport to Ruidoso at the end of the spring semester to decompress. I was studying engineering, and he was pre-med. We were both focused on finishing our bachelor's degrees in four years which meant that the course load could be a little much. Spending a week in the mountains before starting our summer jobs was going to be the perfect break. We arrived late on the first day after a long drive across the length of Texas. My parents' cabin was simple, but we didn't care. It certainly was not roughing it. We set out the next morning for an ambitious hike in the Lincoln National Forest. It was a sunny, late spring day in the mountains, and we were going to cover some territory. I knew of a trail that started just off the road to the Ski Apache resort. As an adolescent, I'd seen the trailhead hundreds of times on the way to the resort, but it was always in winter and my dad was focused on skiing. We never stopped.

Today the two of us Louisiana boys were going to load up with daypacks full of supplies (mostly trail mix and beer) and spend the day tromping through these spectacular peaks. The trail began at about 8000 feet. I felt like John Muir and Edmund Hillary all rolled into one. We headed off into the woods and quickly found that the trail opened into a clearing and then cut almost horizontally across a relatively steep grassy treeless area that skiers would call a "bowl." This section thrilled us. It felt a little dangerous as one false move could send us tumbling down the slope, but the best part was the view. Off in the distance were the Capitan Mountains. Standing on the foothills of Sierra Blanca, looking out over twenty miles of desert at the Capitans made you feel dwarfed by your surroundings, but not in a bad way. Small in a way that gave you a sense of where you fit into this enormous universe.

As I often do on hikes, I proceeded to blabber on with my local knowledge. The Capitan Mountains are a rugged and solitary chain and the home of the original Smokey the Bear. Smokey had been found there as a cub clinging to a tree following the Capitan Gap Fire of 1950. The three-month-old black bear cub was badly burned and was cared for by the forest rangers. His likeness would go on to become the national symbol of forest fire awareness. *Only You Can Prevent Forest Fires.* I felt proud that my adopted hometown had a famous spokesbear that cared about conservation. It was turning into a magical day. The entire slope was in flower and had attracted hummingbirds by the hundreds. The bright little birds were in fine form as they feasted from flower to flower, and the thin mountain air made it harder for them to stay in flight. They sounded like tiny helicopters as they frantically buzzed past our heads in search of nectar.

It was as we re-entered the woods on the other side of the bowl that we saw the pile. It stopped us both in our tracks. There, just off the well worn path, was a large, fresh, steaming pile of bear poop. We could not believe our eyes. In an instant, we both knew what it was. It looked like a pile of dog poop, just about ten times bigger. My first instinct was to tell my joke about how to differentiate black bear poop from grizzly bear poop. For those of you that are not bear aficionados, there is a huge difference between the two species, *ursus americanus* and *ursus arctos horribilis,* and these Latin names imply the story. Black bears live throughout North America, weigh about 150 to 300 pounds, stand about five feet tall and are generally fearful of people. Grizzly bears live in the western US and Canada, weigh 400 to 600 pounds, stand about seven feet tall and, when in doubt, will charge people. Both bear species freak me out, but grizzlies terrify me—and I think this is reasonable.

The bear poop joke goes something like this. How do you differentiate between black bear and grizzly bear scat? They look the same but grizzly bear poop smells like cayenne (from a hiker's attempt to use pepper spray in defense) and contains jingle bells (worn by hikers to warn bears that hikers are approaching). It's a great joke if the timing and delivery are on. As we stared at the poop, our jovial mood faded quickly, and it was no time for even a good joke. From the look of it, this bear must be really close by. We both started to scan the surroundings looking for the bear expecting him to explode from the woods and tear us apart. I started almost hyperventilating while Dave somehow remained calm. I suggested that we immediately head back to the car (which was about a mile away at this point), but Dave wanted to press on. I did too and was impressed by Dave's composure, but my paranoia about bears made hiking on impossible. Soon we were heading back to the car, bummed out that this bear poop had scared us (mostly me) out of the woods on such a remarkable day.

We decided to make the best of the day and go for a hike in the neighborhood near my parents' house. It was a scarcely populated part of the community so a walk often included sighting a mule deer or some other creature unique to the Rockies. We were hyper-alert as we walked along and eventually started talking about snakes and all the close encounters we had with them in Louisiana. You likely know that Louisiana is teeming with reptiles, with the alligator being the star of the show. Every Louisiana kid has stories about seeing a copperhead snake sunbathing on their patio or accidentally stirring up a nest of snakes when out doing yard work with their families. Our tales escalated until I decided to outdo him with my best snake story, and told of the day I was out swimming with a neighbor friend in Cross Lake, about a hundred yards from shore. I should tell you, at this point, that every body of water in the whole state is muddy like you have likely never seen. When you go under the water, you literally cannot see your hand in front of your face. When I first moved to Louisiana, I was reluctant to get in water that was not as clear as a pool, but, eventually,

I got over that fear and started swimming in the muddy water with my friends.

So on this day I was out with my friend AJ on a hot summer day in the cool, murky water when a water moccasin casually swam right between us and stopped. We were treading water about four feet apart when we noticed the snake. AJ had grown up on Cross Lake and was an experienced swimmer, fisher, hunter, and paddler. He had become my nature boy role model. The guy was quite entertaining and a real pyromaniac. I've never seen a person start a fire so quickly or get one going as hot as he could.

I recall the moment we spotted the snake like it happened yesterday. We both noted the snake at the same instant and looked immediately at each other. AJ's look of controlled panic reinforced my suspicion that I was in trouble and about to get my first snake bite. If you have never experienced a water moccasin (also called a cottonmouth), they are not your average snake. Most snakes are afraid of people and only strike when provoked. Shortly after moving to Louisiana, I was warned by another neighbor to watch out for water moccasins. Earlier that year while out fishing, he had one drop from the branch of a cypress tree into his open boat. The snake proceeded to slither around on the bottom of his boat in an attempt to bite him and his fishing companion. As you would expect, it scared the hell out of my neighbor as he attempted to beat the snake with his paddle as he hopped around the boat trying to land a fatal blow. It scared the other guy in the boat so bad that he dove out of the boat and swam to shore. To summarize, water moccasins are aggressive, unpredictable, and you want to steer clear of them.

So here I am watching AJ's face intently as the snake swam between us. I was hoping for a clue as to what I should do. Truth is, he didn't know either. Given the muddy water, all we could see was the head gently swaying back and forth as he propelled himself forward. And then he disappeared underwater. If I thought I was about to get bitten before, I was certain that I would now. When the snake disappeared under water, I looked at AJ again. He was smiling now. Smiling because this whole situation was ridiculous, smiling because our luck was rotten, and smiling because one of us was about to get bitten. We both kept our cool when the snake went under. I began to tread water in the most gentle way I could. I didn't want to provoke the snake and figured that if I went nearly motionless he might just swim on by. We both kept up our gentle treading for what seemed like forever and then, almost simultaneously, we bolted and swam as fast as we could manage back to shore. We thrashed our way on to the bank laughing hysterically, not able to contain our amusement at our lousy luck followed by our amazing luck. A few minutes later, AJ and I went swimming again. I don't recall whether I was motivated by adolescent machismo, or recklessness, or just a love of the lake. Regardless, I would swim in those waters hundreds of times more knowing that they were loaded with snakes and alligators and alligator snapping turtles.

I write of snakes because, to our surprise, Dave and I were about to have another wildlife encounter. As we strolled through the woods—always looking out for bears—I nearly stepped on a rattlesnake. He lay coiled in the leaf litter, perfectly camouflaged. I have to admit that I wasn't really paying attention to where I was stepping until I went to place my foot directly on to the little guy as he gave a quick rattle. The adrenaline kicked in the instant I heard the sound, and I leapt about three feet into the air, missing the snake (thankfully) and scaring the heck out of Dave. We quickly circled back around to inspect the snake as he sat in his coil shaking his rattle. He was a little one, about 18 inches long, and really amazing to look at. We kept our distance and later learned that he was a Western Diamondback based on his pattern and the fact that they are the most common rattler in the region. What a day! Scared off the slopes by fresh bear poop and then nearly bitten by a rattlesnake.

Strangely, I hoped that my return to New Mexico two decades later would be equally eventful, although of course my wife was hoping for a different sort of trip altogether. It's typical to say that places you return to as an adult are smaller and less exciting than you recall them, but that would not be the case with Ruidoso.

It was much bigger than when I left. Its location in the southern Rockies had turned into a popular vacation spot. It had snow skiing in the winter and Quarter Horse racing at Ruidoso Downs in the summer. It maintained its charm with numerous funky motels and a quirky artistic flare similar to the more famous Taos located well north.

As I said, we would be staying at the Thunderbird Motel on one of the main drags in town. To this day, I'm not sure why I chose the place as it did not have much to offer other than its central location. It was the typical roadside motel you would expect in a ski town—no pool or other amenities. In retrospect, I presume that I chose it for the name (and the price). When I saw their logo with a majestic image of the mythological bird, I was hooked. I'll state right now that there is a very big difference between the real thunderbird and the stories about it, and this kind of commercialization aimed at getting people into motels and restaurants, but the advertisement worked in the way that advertising always does. We'd been to the Museum of Civilization in Ottawa and seen the indigenous peoples' carvings of totem poles not long before. They entranced me with their combination of size, craftsmanship, nature, and symbolism. The carved killer whales were pretty amazing, but it's hard to beat the Thunderbird.

Many cultures throughout the world include a large mythological bird in their folklore. These birds are always enormous, but their relationship with First Nations people is widely varied. Some tribes see them as the bringer of rain. To them, the name is literal. The thunder they hear is caused by the bird flapping its wings. Lightning would emanate from their flight feathers or from snakes on their chest and the life-giving rain would follow. Other stories describe the Thunderbird as a protector who battled a great water serpent in an effort to keep the world safe. Thunderbirds are also common in creation myths. Their epic fight with mythic killer whales was the explanation for the prairie found on the Olympic peninsula. Other myths describe them as vengeful gods capable of destroying a whole tribe for disobedience.

Always the scientist, I looked for a logical explanation for the indigenous tales of these amazing birds. Could First Nations people just be seeing enormous birds and ascribing them magical powers to explain natural phenomena like thunder and lightning? My fascination with California Condors made me start to picture them with lightning surging from their wingtips. Paleontologists have speculated that a prehistoric bird known as *Teratornis merriami* may be an explanation of the Thunderbird lore. This species of teratorn lived in North America until about ten thousand years ago and would have coexisted with tribal ancestors. These birds were colossal, weighing over 30 pounds and with wingspans up to 12 feet. They would have dwarfed the eagles and vultures of today many times over.

Bigger still was the *Argentiva* that went extinct six to eight million years ago. It stood over four feet tall, weighed roughly 180 pounds, and had a wingspan of 33 feet—definitely a thunderous bird. The Argentiva is thought to be the largest bird to ever fly. Some have speculated that the Thunderbird could even be a Pterodactyl, but they have been extinct for 65 million years. It should be noted that a pterodactyl sighting was reported in the *Tombstone Epigraph* in 1890 in Arizona when it was fired upon by a group of gunslingers. Critics note that it was probably just a slow news day, but the article (that includes photos) is worth reading and available online.

My journey back to the mountains of southern New Mexico was starting to feel like a pilgrimage. After my recent experiences with cryptids and my immersion into Polynesian language and mythology, I returned to Ruidoso with a heightened awareness of my small place in humankind. Southern New Mexico is home to the Mescalero Apache reservation. It spans a huge section of the mountain range and includes the Ski Apache resort, the Inn of the Mountain Gods Resort, and much of the region surrounding Ruidoso and Cloudcroft. The Mescaleros have long been one of the wealthiest tribes in the country and their influence on the culture of the region is strong. As a child growing up out west, I was fascinated by their traditional stories, and, as an adult interested in environmental conservation, I was drawn to their respect for nature and how their folklore tied them to the earth.

Once settled at the Thunderbird Motel, I immediately wanted to start exploring and showing my wife and son the town and region. The mountains were even more beautiful than I had remembered. I'd moved to New York over a decade ago and spent a lot of my free time exploring the Appalachian Mountains of the east. I love the Adirondacks, the Catskills, and the Allegany Mountains, but they are just not on the same scale as the Rockies.

My first impulse was to go fishing, which was odd considering that I had not gone fishing in decades. Also, we didn't bring any equipment and would have to get licences. Add to that we did not have a place to cook the fish we might catch (and that I don't eat fish), and we soon decided that this was a stupid idea, indeed. What I actually wanted was to walk along a mountain stream and listen to the water and the birds. Fortunately, that turned out to be really simple since the Grindstone Lake Trail started just on the edge of downtown Ruidoso.

It was a relatively easy trail and refreshing to be out in these familiar woods again. The more you hike, the more you appreciate how different the flora in different places can be. There are places in North Louisiana that are so dense with vegetation that you really need a machete at times. And of course, there are those darn snakes that make you measure every step you take. In northern Ontario, the growing season is so short that trees that are hundreds of years old are only ten feet tall. The ground coverage in these high desert mountains was just right. You were surrounded by trees but did not have to fight your way through brush if you wanted to explore off trail. These were my Goldilocks Woods—they were just right.

It was an invigorating hike. My amateur botanist wife loved trying to identify all these new plants. I was loving the view and trying to identify all the western bird varieties that I had not seen in years while hoping to spot a roadrunner. And my son, Niles, could not get enough of my stories about his wacky grandfather pretending to lose control of his car on icy mountain roads. We had so much fun that we decided that hiking would become our daily outing and started planning our trip for the following day during that evening's dinner.

We decided that the next hike would be ambitious. Years ago, I had climbed Sierra Blanca with friends starting from the Ski Apache resort parking lot. We thought that a repeat of this would be best for us as it provided a good base and the views at the terminus would likely be spectacular. My kid was enthusiastic about the hike. We had hiked some of the High Peaks of the Adirondacks the previous summer, and the thought of climbing a mountain over 12,000 feet had him motivated. My wife, on the other hand, wisely had contingency plans when she noticed that the hike was described as "strenuous" and started at 9700 ft. Our vacation the previous summer had shown us both our limits when hiking in high altitudes given that we were acclimated to essentially sea level. She left the motel that morning expecting to bail on the hike and likely take the ski gondola up to a neighboring peak and spend some time looking for, and photographing, the native plants.

As expected, my wife decided about a mile into the hike that this had been fun, but that the gondola was a way smarter option. The "men" could carry on, and she would use technology to get to the top. Niles and I set off with purpose to climb the tallest peak in the southern Rockies. Hiking came naturally to him as we'd been hiking with him since he could hold his head up in a baby backpack. Now as a teenager, he was really fit and could probably out hike me. My only concern was that he would try something stupid and sprain something miles from the car. Mostly the hike was a gradual climb up an intermediate-level ski run, wide and smooth with easy, grassy footing. We walked along at a brisk pace until the atmosphere started to get thinner. Climbing a 2300-foot displacement over several miles at this altitude was going to be rather challenging. I had skied down this run hundreds of times as an adolescent. I had learned to ski at the time of the 1976 Olympics, and my idol quickly became Austrian skier Franz Klammer when he won the downhill. As a thrill-seeking boy, going fast was all that mattered, and I fearlessly pointed my skis down the slope and tried to go as fast as I could. I wiped out a lot but never seriously hurt myself. Our path up the mountain was not steep enough to qualify for an Olympic downhill course, but my many runs down the slope were on my mind as we hiked along.

Eventually we made it out of the valley and into the bowl. This ski run was known as Apache Bowl and if you followed the chair lift towers straight up the hill, you ended up at the top of Lookout Mountain with a panoramic view of the high desert and the gypsum dunes of the White Sands National Monument. The dunes were created by runoff from the adjacent Sacramento Mountains, and as a kid I thought of them as the world's largest beach, although it lacked an ocean. But now my son and I veered to the left toward the peak of Sierra Blanca. How I loved that mountain! It towered 5500 feet over the desert plain, could be seen from over 100 miles away and was actually the remains of a volcano. It had been named by Spanish settlers (obviously) but was known as Dziãgais'â-ní (Sacred Mountain) to the Apaches. (Apache actually means "enemy" and it's not surprising that's not how the Apache people refer to themselves, which I understand is *Ndee, Inday,* or *Dine'é.*) We had acquired the pass required by the tribe to allow us to climb the peak this week. A group of crows (known as a murder) started to make a real racket as we entered the bowl. The mountain crows always seem larger than your average crow. We watched them for a while and decided that they were not large enough to be ravens. (This led me to ramble on about the role the raven has played in legends. I'd been reading a lot of that stuff lately.)

We soon passed the 11,000-foot level, above the treeline and the going became a little tougher due to the thinning oxygen. We pressed on, willing to take it a little slower and admire the view. As we walked out of the bowl and on to the crestline between Dziãgais'â-ní and Lookout Mountain, the view to the west became doubly remarkable. As usual, I started to blabber on about the high desert view. Not only did it contain White Sands, but it also had Alamogordo, the site of the first detonation of a nuclear bomb (the

Trinity Site). It disturbed me to wonder what the first mushroom cloud looked like over this lovely valley. New Mexico still has tons of federal research institutes and is home to the highest percentage of PhDs of any state in the country.

We decided to rest and have lunch. I needed to catch my breath and eating seemed like a good excuse. I generally splurge when it comes to hiking meals. Food always seems to taste better when surrounded by natural beauty. Past hikes have included wine, craft ales, fancy cheeses, hummus, olive tapenade, pastries, and more. I've been considering buying a hiking ice cream maker that somehow stirs up dessert as you bounce along the trail. Today would be simple—some deli sandwiches we'd picked up on the way to the resort. I skipped the beer I had packed as the high altitude was already making me a little loopy. We then pressed on toward the peak as it teased us from the modest clouds that clung to it. Walking the crestline was a little tricky. On the surface it did not appear that dangerous but clearly a wrong step could send you sliding down the mountainside.

We were navigating around a large solitary rock when it happened. The footing on the west side (the far side) of the crestline gave way and started a rockslide. We both fell to our backsides and started down the hill almost like sledding. But this wasn't nearly as much fun as sledding and soon we were picking up speed and getting clobbered by larger and larger rocks. We came to rest about 300 yards from the crestline and it was clear that we were both injured and a long way from help. My right leg had taken a serious blow and I was pretty sure that it was broken just above the ankle. I was more concerned about my son who had taken a rock to his chest. By the pain that he was in, I suspected that he had broken a couple ribs. He was able to take full breaths but each one caused him significant discomfort. Breathing at this altitude can be hard enough without a rib injury.

I tried not to panic. I had brought my trusty walking stick so I felt I would be able to use it as a crutch and make it down the mountain. We took a nearby branch and started fashioning a splint for my ankle using a windbreaker I kept in my bag. The hardest part of our journey back to the car would be climbing up the western slope of the mountain to the crestline so that we could begin the walk down to the resort. My biggest concern was that not many people hike all the way to the peak of Sierra Blanca so waiting for someone to help us out could take a while, or all day. After fixing my splint, we made an attempt to climb up the hill. The footing was terrible—it was a rock slide after all. We would struggle up the hill for a while to make it only a few feet. Our efforts were feeling fruitless and my son was getting really frustrated. It was pretty clear that his rib injury was causing significant pain, but he did not want to admit it.

We would go on with our attempts to climb out for several hours. Your mind starts to race at times like this. My favorite part of *Backpacker* magazine is the section on how to survive an unexpected event while out in the wilderness. It is often about some guy out for a lengthy trail run who takes a wrong turn and ends up wandering the desert for three days until a helicopter finds him, or a family rafting party flips over in rapids and spends a week climbing out of a gorge. So here we were, injured, stuck and exhausted in the middle of nowhere. My first thought was the anxiety we were going to cause my wife. I am an annoyingly timely person and our return to the main resort being late by even a couple hours would start her asking the resort staff for help. In addition to everything else, I could not get cell phone service at this remote location. Fortunately, it was a warm day so I was not too worried about hypothermia if we had to stay out overnight, and a search party would not have a hard time finding us as we stayed true to the trail, apart from sliding several hundred yards off the crestline.

We continued to struggle our way up the hill to the crestline and eventually made it to within about twenty yards of the top when the altitude and exhaustion really kicked in. I had to rest and we decided that it was a good time to have "dinner." It was around 6 p.m. and sunset was about an hour away. The view was fantastic as ever, but the wide expanse of mountain and desert below did make the point that we were very alone up here. I recalled the hundreds of colorful, desert sunsets I had seen with my family growing up in El Paso. We opened the daypack and sized up our supplies. We drank some water. Fortunately, we were adequately stocked on that, and we ate the remains of the granola bars and dried fruit, noting that it was better to carry them in our stomachs than on our backs. I located my camping headlamps and was glad that I left a pair in the bag just in case. We would need them tonight as we made our way down the slope in the dark. I suggested that we lay down and rest a bit before making one last push to the top and then, triumphantly, down the mountain to safety. (I was trying to stay positive for my son.)

I'm not sure how long I dozed when I was awoken by a tremendous breeze. At first, I thought that I was dreaming when the rocks shifted underneath me and I felt a strong force grab me around my hips and shoulders. As I gained my bearings, I looked at my son levitating off of the rock slide and up into the air. As you know by now, I have an active imagination, and my first reaction was to see this as some sort of biblical ascent to heaven, but there were no harps, parting of clouds, or lights from above. So my next thought was that we were being abducted by aliens! Again, my brain works in strange ways. (Off by about one hundred miles to the east lies Roswell, New Mexico, home of the famous UFO wreck from the 1940s. When you add Roswell with the nuclear test site near Alamogordo, Holoman Air Force Base and White Sands Missile Range, there is definitely an otherworldly feel to the region and may even be some strange objects flying around in the desert sky. When we were kids, my brother was convinced that he and his friends saw a hovering spacecraft over the Organ Mountains north of El Paso. My father, then a colonel in the army, dismissed the sighting as a new surveillance flare that the army was probably working on.)

As I was lifted up off the rock slide by some invisible force, I was pretty sure this had nothing to do with a surveillance flare. I felt securely held by my hips and torso as if a giant bird was carrying me. The intermittent downward breeze was intense as I was flown up over the ridgeline. I twisted around in near panic looking for Niles and spotted him about fifty yards away floating over the crestline suspended in the same posture in which I found myself. Once I topped the ridge, the downward breezes stopped and we started a smooth glide across the sloping bowl down into the valley of the ski resort. My hands were free so I reached up to feel for what was holding so firmly on to my hips and torso to discover that it appeared to be the feet of an enormous bird of prey. I stared at my hands in wonder as they traced out what I could best describe as a pair of invisible taloned feet cradling my body. We swooped in close to Niles as if the "birds" were checking in on each other, and I called to him: "Stay calm. I think we're being rescued." It was about a minute later that his "guardian" let out a sharp crackling sound that could pass for a thunderclap. I had just started to enjoy our rapid descent down the mountain as I reflected on Charlie and his grandfather flying with Willy Wonka in his glass elevator when the crackling call was uttered. It brought me back to reality and the danger we were in if we fell from such a height.

Eventually, we descended onto a meadow at the top of a hill overlooking the main buildings of the ski resort where we were gently dropped into the tall, unmown grass. And with a series of powerful breezes our rescuers powered away. We struggled to our feet to gaze down the moderate hill at the resort complex and nearly empty parking lot. As if by magic, a young employee, about 20 years old, pulled out of the woods driving a pickup truck and asked us if we needed help. Clearly we were a sad looking pair. We thanked her for her concern and limped into the vehicle. As is often the case at Ski Apache, the young woman was a member of a local tribe and asked us how we ended up on top of the hill in such a state. Once again, I recounted another ridiculous tale involving occurrences that no logical person would believe. The young woman, who I will call Jill, listened intently and respectfully to the tale which was corroborated by Niles. We both struggled over how to describe the creatures that lifted us from the rock slide on the far side of the mountain and explain how we could not see them but could feel their presence, touch them, hear them, and feel the wind they generated. As we concluded our story, a powerful crash of lightning could be seen up on a neighboring hill followed by a roll of thunder. It was a cloudless evening.

A huge smile broke across the young woman's face and she said: "You have been visited by thunderbirds. They have taken pity on your misfortune and acted to save your lives. They care for us and bring us rain and protect us from the water serpent Uktena." She said this as we arrived in the parking lot adjacent to our rental car where my wife was waiting. She was pleased to see us but shocked by our sorry state. The first aid station at the resort that treats injured skiers was closed in the off season. Our new friend gave us directions to the Lincoln Medical Center where our injuries could be addressed, but ended by giving me the phone and address for her father, the spiritual leader of the Mescaleros. "Call us when you are fixed up. My dad will want to speak with you tonight."

The medical care we received at the Lincoln County Medical Center was remarkably prompt. In retrospect, it's not surprising that taking x-rays for Niles' broken ribs and splinting my ankle would be routine in a ski town. As we left the hospital, I called Jill's father and was invited to his home, which was only a twenty minute ride. He greeted us in the yard of his modest home on the reservation and showed us to a lovely patio with an amazing view of the mountain. He inquired about our health and the treatments we had just received and then related a story from years ago when he wiped out on a four wheeler many miles from home.

He was a weathered, rugged-looking fifty-ish Apache man with short brush cut hair. Lean and well-muscled, he could have passed for one of the drill sergeants I had known from my youth growing up on army bases. But when he spoke, it was clear that he chose his words with the care of someone connected with the spiritual world. We talked at length about the experience with my son that day, and I recounted my recent experiences in cryptozoological medicine. In short, his understanding of the hidden side of the natural world blew my mind. Here was a man who had clearly experienced "vision quests." I feel that to relate our conversation at length would be a violation of the trust he placed in me and the knowledge that he so freely shared. But I will relay his thoughts on our experiences on the mountain earlier that day.

He assured me that we had indeed been rescued by thunderbirds and commented that he commonly sees them while exploring the local mountains. He related that thunderbirds can cloak themselves when desired so that to "non-believers" they would seem invisible. Niles suggested that this was akin to only being able to see Thestrals in Harry Potter's world if you had seen death. Our host was very pleased by the Potter analogy.

My wife took the opportunity to embarrass our son by saying: "I prefer to think that it was a stork that brought my baby to me a second time." This comment irritated our son but brought great joy to the rest of us. Birds have been part of the folklore of nearly every society on earth. Europeans have used storks for over a century to explain where babies come from, but this idea was popularized by Hans Christian Andersen with his story "The Storks."

Thunderbird—best approximation

But on a more spiritual level, our host wanted to discuss the Dalai Lama and the role that the Black-necked Crane plays in Tibetan Buddhism. He described the thunderbirds as something similar to an enormous condor—all black with the powerful red and yellow head of a raptor. Thunderbirds had inhabited the region for as long as known history. They are considered to be shepherds of the tribe and the bringer of rain. He often saw them during storms with lightning emanating from their flight feathers. He joked that Apache legend was not as colorful as that of the tribes of the Pacific Northwest where thunderbirds waged epic battles with the Great Horned Sea Serpent or with the ancestors of the killer whale. His thunderbirds just mostly brought rain.

We asked him to thank the thunderbirds on our behalf and he told me that thanks were not needed. He suggested that his spirit friends had been watching over us since we returned to the mountains. My efforts to help magical creatures had not gone unnoticed in the "hidden world" (as he called it), and carrying us down the mountain to safety was "payback" for all I had done over the years to help the creatures of the world, both seen and unseen. Words can't explain how that made me feel. I think that everyone wants a fairy godmother, but having your own guardian thunderbird was way cooler.

We spent the evening chatting with his family and would have been content to stay there for days or longer. It had become clear to all of us that there was much to learn about the world around us and that I was going to need a wiser man for guidance.

With our injuries, the rest of our time in southern New Mexico was less adventurous than the start of our trip. We drove out to the Capitan Mountains to visit the birthplace of Smokey the Bear and went south to Carlsbad Caverns to witness the evening migration of millions of Mexican free-tailed bats (*Tadarida brasiliensis*) as they flew off to hunt for the night. I spent most of my time watching the sky wishing to spot a thunderbird in flight.

CHAPTER EIGHT

THERE HAVE BEEN A LOT of coincidences in my life recently. Before the chupacabra, the sasquatch, the plesiosaur, and so much more weirdness had occurred, I had made plans to attend a veterinary conference in Scotland—home of the Loch Ness monster (along with thousands of other remarkable attractions). The trip had been the brainchild of my friend and large animal veterinarian, Jan Foreman. Jan and I had become friends years previously when I had volunteered to represent the local vet society at the Erie County Fair.

Our county fair is rather large and has the typical display of cows, goats, horses, pigs, chickens, and various domesticated animals that city slickers expect to gawk at when they go to the country. Jan (large animal) and I (small animal) met when we were paired to look after the animals one morning at the fair and would go on to serve together on a number of veterinary boards over the next decade or so. I loved hanging out with Jan. She is probably the most direct and down-to-earth person I have met. Her unique take on life and off-the-wall sense of humor made her someone I would search out when in a roomful of colleagues. I like to joke that she has no filter. I always find her charming but she has surely rubbed some the wrong way.

It was during a happy hour prior to the Western New York Veterinary Medical Association winter meeting that she invited me to join her and some of her vet school classmates at the annual veterinary conference at the University of Glasgow's veterinary college in Scotland. She was really looking forward to going and made a good pitch for me to go along. The travel and hotel rates were outstanding and the options for excursions were right up my alley: whiskey tours, sailing tours, Viking tours, and even a backpacking tour through the Scottish Highlands.

I had been to Scotland years before, shortly after graduating from vet school, and enjoyed myself thoroughly. It reminded me of Newfoundland but with a different history. My employer gives me an annual travel stipend for conferences, and so as I thought it over, this trip started to make a lot of sense. I could get away, earn some continuing education credits, have most of the costs covered by my employer, and take some side trips. How could I not go?

I started planning this trip before the chupacabra incident, and the other cryptid experiences unfolded in rapid fashion. As travel to Scotland approached, I started to have second thoughts. I am a worrier by nature. I think I get it from my mother's side. Both she and her mother could work themselves into nervous wrecks about travel plans—especially any kind of family reunion. Weather, illness, accommodations, baggage ... these are the things we dwell on. And with the recent events of my life, I could now add that out of nowhere I could find myself having to care for a griffon or a dragon or a pterodactyl.

We planned to fly from Toronto to Glasgow and spend three days at the conference. At the end of the conference, we were going to take a backpacking trip for several days on the northern part of the West Highland Way. Having been to Scotland previously, I took comfort in knowing that Glasgow and the Highland Way were a good distance from Loch Ness, that center of alleged paranormal activity. I'd been to Loch Ness and Inverness on my previous trip to Scotland so I didn't feel like I was missing out on a sightseeing opportunity, and frankly, as stated previously, I had my suspicions that strange forces were at work drawing me, my father, my brother, my cousin and who knows what other relatives into encounters with cryptids in need. I had developed a theory that the whole extended family was prone to supernatural experiences, but that the rest of them were concealing the truth.

I was intent on not getting sucked into another stressful experience with a strange and potentially dangerous creature. This was going to be a relaxing and educational trip. Besides, there have been no reported chupacabra sightings in northern climates and the UK has been sasquatch-free for centuries. I would stay away from the Loch and the seashore, and my biggest threat would be a fairy or two. Though sadly, I still hadn't seen a fairy yet.

Loch Ness Monster
Nessiteras rhombopteryx

Returning to Scotland was oddly familiar. On my previous trip there, I had met up with my college roommate Dave and his friend, Donald Owens. Dave had just started working as a psychiatrist in Boston and met Donald through a nurse at his hospital. Both the nurse and Donald were born and raised in Scotland. Donald was a microbiologist on sabbatical in Boston. He loved traveling around America, and Dave became his tour guide to the northeast. Over several months, they spent many weekends together trekking around New England checking out the sites. This was all new for Dave as well, having grown up in Louisiana. When Donald returned to his home in Dundee, Scotland, he had Dave promise that he would allow him to return the favor by having him stay at his house and take him around his native Scotland.

It seemed logical that, after my time in Newfoundland, I would befriend a scientist from Scotland. The two regions are remarkably similar. Both are islands in the North Atlantic with cold, rainy climates and similar inhabitants. Obviously the Scottish history stretches back much farther and has a rich past full of royalty and rebellion, while Newfoundland maintains its culture as a rugged, working-class outpost. Donald had grown up in a working class section of Edinburgh where his scholastic skill earned him entrance into a prestigious high school. He would go on to earn a PhD in microbiology and work as an instructor at the medical school in Dundee.

I joked previously that veterinarians often don't want to share their profession with people they meet, because we will get pelted with stories about somebody's mother having a twenty-two year-old cat or, worse, be asked how best to housebreak a dog. With Donald, it was different. We met the first time just a few years after the Mad Cow scare in the UK was front page news. As a microbiologist in the UK, he was really knowledgeable about the disease. He was eager to discuss the topic with a veterinarian, and we had a good time predicting what the course of the disease would be. We continued to bond over our nerdiness by discussing Dolly, the cloned sheep. I had forgotten that Dolly was created in Scotland. Traveling around Scotland with Donald was a blast. He seemed to know every pub in the country, told great stories about the Stone of Scone and other aspects of Scottish history, and did hysterical impressions of the variety of Scottish accents. He was amused and horrified by Groundskeeper Willie from *The Simpsons*, which pleased Dave and me to no end.

On my return to Scotland, I had a number of items on my agenda, not the least being the desire to try what the country had to drink. I realize that I am starting to sound like an alcoholic here, but I do love alcoholic beverages. In fact, I love just about everything about it, especially the art of making it. My fascination began in grad school when I started homebrewing beer with my professor Robert. A number of people in the ocean physics department made their own beer, and soon I was becoming a connoisseur. I would go on over the next decade to make ale, lager, wine, mead, cyser, sake, rum, brandy, absinthe and just anything you can think of. Fermentation is a magical combination of biology, physics, chemistry, culture, history, and craftsmanship that fascinates many people. Later in my life, it would combine with my wife's love of gardening, and our yard would come to have trellises adorned with hops, an arbor covered in grapevines, and a garden with a variety of brewing herbs. My love of fermentation was so strong, in fact, that I seriously considered entering the UC Davis program for a degree in viticulture and enology instead of going to vet school. Vet school would win out, but my love of using yeast to turn agricultural products into a delicious beverage will never die.

Oystercatcher
Haemotopus ostralegus

After the educational sessions had concluded on the first afternoon of the conference, my new friends and I spent the evening at a pub along the River Kelvin in the city of Glasgow. We chose the pub for two reasons. First, the river was named after Lord Kelvin—the eighteenth century scientist that the Kelvin temperature scale is named after. He was a hero of mine and had been a professor at the University of Glasgow. But what pleased me almost as much was that the pub's beer selection was extensive. While in Scotland previously, Donald had served me a pint of Dark Island Ale from a brewery on the Orkney Islands. Its malty, nutty qualities made it delicious then, and it seemed even better now served naturally conditioned from a cask. As we finished our meal and a few more beers, we started to exchange stories from our work lives, as people from a common profession tend to do. My new friends were all large animal practitioners, and, frankly, large animal vet stories are better than the small animal ones. The settings are better, typically in some weird barn or out in a pasture, and the animals are bigger and thus a little more intimidating. And their clients are just more eccentric—although there is a certain breed of cat people who can compete with the best of them.

Not wanting to be outdone (and fortified by the Dark Island Ale), I started to share my chupacabra story. I'd had a mixed response to the story from my family previously, but I figured what the heck. Of course, nobody believed it, especially Jan. Don't get me wrong, they loved the story and ate up every word. They just thought I was pulling their legs. So I shared the sasquatch story, and here is where it got a little weird because Jan knew Marble Ridge Farm. She'd been to their stables countless times as a large animal vet. The owners (Jessica and Harold) were her friends and clients. Everyone in Buffalo had heard of the sasquatch sighting, and Jan had recently heard rumors in the rural communities that she served that a poacher had tried to kill the beast. As I laid out the tale and our efforts at the Buffalo Zoo hospital to save him, you could tell that she wanted to believe me but just couldn't bring herself to take the plunge. I would go on to share the other parts of my life not protected by my confidentiality agreement with IUCNNR: Lake Erie's Bessie, the sasquatch behind my parent's house in Louisiana, my father and Dr. Winston with the jackalope in the Arizona desert, and my cousin and the yeti in northern Ontario.

We all had a great time laughing about these stories. I don't know that I convinced any of them, but it certainly made for a pub night that we would all remember. For once, my family's odd stories at the dinner table did not cause patrons nearby to move to other tables in disgust, but instead some locals joined in and laughed along. As the evening wrapped up, my colleagues pointed out that Loch Ness was only a couple hours' drive away and that I should head over in case Nessie needed my help. Maybe I could stop by a hardware store on the way to get properly stocked. They were falling over themselves laughing at their own wit. At this point, I made it clear that I was out of the cryptid-rescuing business. I joked that I'd had a priest in Buffalo exorcise me of the problem, much the same as Jim had done with his home along the Newfoundland fairy path.

The rest of the conference was pretty standard—a few hours of lecture each morning followed by sightseeing around Glasgow. I left Glasgow really impressed by how the city blended its modern, cutting-edge architecture with historic preservation. I'd become quite interested in historic architecture and preservation since moving to Buffalo. During Buffalo's boom days about a century ago, influential architects, such as Frederick Law Olmsted, Calvert Vaux, H.H. Richardson, Frank Lloyd Wright and Louis Sullivan, came to Buffalo to create the park system and a number of their masterpieces. And thankfully, most of these works have been preserved.

A few of us vets headed north to spend some days hiking the northern section of the West Highland Way. On my previous visit to Scotland, Dave, Donald, and I had met a pair of Americans in a pub who were in the middle of backpacking the entire West Highland Way from Glasgow to the terminus in Fort William. Dave and I thought this was really cool. We had hiked portions of the Appalachian Trail back in the States, but hiking 100 miles through the Scottish countryside, complete with moors, highlands and distilleries, sounded amazing, although we wondered how good our tent and foul weather gear would need to be.

This hiking trip across Scotland, however, was going to be "slackpacking" at its finest. True backpacking is when you take everything you need (tent, food, clothes, etc.) and carry it all on your back for the whole journey, living in the elements, eating dehydrated food, rarely bathing. On the other end of the comfort level, slackpackers carry only what they need for the day's hike. At the start of each day, they put their luggage in a van and make plans to meet their belongings at the end of the day's hike at a hotel, take a shower, have a nice meal and sleep in a real bed. Both ends of the spectrum have their merits. I enjoy time in nature in all its forms, but this trip was going to be comfy.

Our itinerary was going to have three hiking legs—Inverovan to Kingshouse, Kingshouse to Kinlochleven, and wrap up with the last leg from Kinlochleven to Fort William, hopefully with a quick trip up the UK's tallest mountain, Ben Nevis. There would be five of us in the hiking group: me, Jan, her vet school roommate Rebecca, a general practitioner from rural Scotland named Irwin, and an anesthesiologist from the vet school, Edgar. We had befriended Edgar at one of our happy hours and he had decided to come along with these crazy Americans. He was a city kid from London who'd ended up working in the vet school in Glasgow after his residency training. He'd been living in Glasgow for a few years but had not left the city much. When he learned that these three colleagues had travelled across the Atlantic Ocean to hike a trail that was practically in his backyard, he decided to tag along.

The bus ride from Glasgow was uneventful. Leaving a large city and heading out into the wilderness has always given me a feeling of liberation. I like people in general, but there is something about getting out into open spaces that is invigorating. The bus dropped us off in Inveroran. Apart from a few big cities, Scotland is rather rural and seems to be made up of lovely old towns and countryside. As we stood by the roadside trying to get our bearings and locate the hotel that headquartered the shuttle service, I was eager to get on my way. I'd been reading about the West Highland Way for weeks and could not wait to get out in the wild and start bird-watching. The tourist information had photos of a slew of birds including Golden Eagles, and I'd never seen a Golden Eagle in the wild. They don't live in the Eastern U.S., where I have spent my entire adult life. Wouldn't it be ironic if the first time I saw this bird so associated with the Rocky Mountains was on a hiking trip in Scotland? I recalled the first Oystercatcher I spotted years ago while driving near Inverness on the other coast of Scotland. I was so excited at checking this bird off my life list that my car mates (Dave and Donald) were a little annoyed by my exuberance. I would go on to see about twenty more Oystercatchers before the car trip ended. Dave and Donald would bust out laughing at each of the last ten we spotted toward the end of that trip.

After dropping off our gear for the baggage transfer, we were off to the trailhead. I felt a little under-prepared as I did not have my trusty walking stick. It had been given to me years ago by my parents who had purchased it in the gift shop at Big Bend National Park on the Texas-Chihuahua border. Made from the spire of a cactus, the stick was the perfect length for me, lightweight and really strong. It gave my balance a sense of security, helped in climbing and descending hills, had proved useful in fending off aggressive dogs, and made me feel cooler when out on the trail. As chance would have it, as we approached the trailhead, I spotted a hiking stick leaning against a fence that was remarkably like my own. Hikers often do this. They look out for each other. There is a code: You share food, water, knowledge, shelter and stories. Someone had left the stick for me and, added to my well-worn hiking boots, trusty binoculars and recently purchased *RSPB Handbook of Scottish Birds*, I was ready for some hiking.

As we started down the trail, I intentionally toned down my enthusiasm knowing that as a morning person I can be irritating at times. My first impulse, as I have said before, is always to start rambling about whatever pops into my head. I was going to play it cool this time and take in the scenery. This was easy to do as we were going to be walking through a remarkable wilderness known as the Rannoch Moor. I'm still not sure what exactly makes a moor a moor. I guess you know one when you see one. There were lots of moors in Newfoundland—treeless, grassy, water laden undeveloped landscape. Newfoundlanders called them "barrens," but they were anything but. Moors are effectively wildlife preserves, and the Rannoch Moor was known for sightings of the Hen Harrier, one of Scotland's most high-profile birds of prey. I kept the binoculars and book handy.

We pressed on in silence. It was better this way. We'd all spent the last several days surrounded by people and being inundated with medical information at the conference. Enjoying the fresh air and panoramic views occupied us until we made it to the Kingshouse Hotel. It had been the perfect walk, and now we would relax at a lovely hotel along the River Etive with spectacular views of the Buachaille Etive Mòr mountain. At dinner, Jan decided to entertain us by clowning around with monster talk. Irwin and Edgar had not been present at the session at the pub along the River Kelvin and needed to be introduced to my tales of cryptozoology. The usual hilarity ensued—at my expense, of course. I had found that it was more fun to discuss my experiences with scientists and veterinarians than with the general public. They, of course, wanted to joke around with the preposterousness of my claims, but eventually I could draw them in with the details of the medicine, or the genetics, or the conservational aspects. I had come to the conclusion that good scientists are just more curious than the average person.

It was during the evening's discussion that I learned that Edgar had studied in Newfoundland. His undergrad degree was in biology with an interest in marine mammals. We'd lived somewhat parallel lives, and he had even spent a summer interning with a marine biologist at MUN a few years after I graduated. I kept the mermaid stories under wraps, but we started to talk at length about the fairies. Irwin, the Scotsman, joined in. Having grown up in rural Scotland near Aberdeen, he'd heard numerous mysterious tales of fairies from his grandmother. Listening to the two of them, it was clear that there were parallels in Newfoundland and Scottish fairy tales. We turned the tables on Jan and started to warn her to watch out for the fairies. We noted that fairies appeared to be attracted to the innocent and the simple-minded. Without missing a beat, she picked a dinner roll off the table and placed it in her pocket. "For the walk tomorrow," she said to our howling laughter. The ice was broken. This traveling party had really begun.

After a proper Scottish breakfast the next morning (I skipped the blood pudding, bangers and smoked fish but enjoyed the porridge, beans, tea, and broiled tomato), we were off for the next leg. It was only going to be nine miles to the next hotel in Kinlochleven. That's an easy walk even by slackpacking standards. It would include a zig-zagging climb up the Devil's Staircase but most of it was a level walk through Glen Etive. We took it leisurely and spent most of the day in conversation, discussing politics the majority of the time. When not discussing wildlife, domestic or otherwise, I've spent much of my life discussing politics and welcomed the chance to talk with a couple people from the UK with very different life experiences. I recalled the numerous conversations I'd had in grad school in Newfoundland in the 1990s. The province was going through genuine upheaval as Canada was looking to finalize the constitution they started in 1867 but never fully ratified. It sounds crazy, but the province of Quebec never officially signed on, and Newfoundland was actually a British commonwealth until 1948 when they joined Canada after the turmoil of World War II.

As an outsider, I enjoyed watching Canadians spar over the rights of various provinces and whether Quebec was a "distinct society." I played the devil's advocate most of the time and insisted that if Newfoundland wanted to break off from Canada that they could always join the U.S. as their premier Joey Smallwood had bargained for sixty years previously. As we passed a site along the trail where the village scenes for the movie *Braveheart* had been filmed, the conversation turned to Scottish independence. About a decade previously, the Scottish people had voted to establish a Scottish Parliament that would give them home rule while keeping the country a part of the UK. This seemed like a perfect compromise to me. Scotland was a lovely country and appeared to be thriving to me, but the old resentments of colonization are strong.

It was at this time that I made a joke regarding the royal crest of Great Britain and how lions and unicorns should be able to get along. The Americans in the group had no idea what I was talking about, while the British veterinarians thought this was rather comical. Fortunately for the purpose of illustration, Irwin happened to have a royal crest sewn on to his day pack. Travelers often sew on badges to identify their bags and act as conversation starters. He set down the bag so that we could admire this strange piece of art that was carefully designed to represent his nation's identity. It consisted of a number of Fleur de Lis, several stretched out lions in profile, a voluptuous topless woman's torso superimposed on a harp, a larger lion with prominent nails and a unicorn rearing up and looking rather menacing but still chained to the ground. In addition, the caption of the crest said in French (*not* English, I'd like to note) that the royal family has the divine right to rule.

This was clearly one messed up country to require such a hodgepodge of symbols to represent its national identity. Irwin proceeded to explain that the lion had long been a symbol of England even though lions have never lived in England. He then noted that the unicorn was the symbol of Scotland and that lions and unicorns were sworn enemies. I was happy to have him take the lead on this discussion of mythology and cryptozoology. Unicorns hold a special place in human history as a mythological creature. The first mention of unicorns in literature goes back to ancient China where the mother of Confucius met a unicorn (called a *Kirin*) who informed her that her child would be special. It should be noted that the actual genus of unicorns is thought to be a variant of the antelope and has divided into three distinct species (Asian, *Monoceros orientalis;* Middle Eastern, *Monoceros tyrannus*; and European, *Monoceros europus*). The book *Dragons and Unicorns: A Natural History* by Paul and Karin Johnsgard is an excellent reference on the natural and cultural history of unicorns.

If you are thinking that unicorns are adorable creatures like My Little Pony but with a tusk, you could not be more wrong. First, unicorns are not horses. They are ruminants with a cloven hoof. This means that horses and unicorns have different leg and hoof structure and a profoundly different gastrointestinal tract. The evolutionary thinking is that many years ago a creature related to the modern antelope evolved a single, large central horn (a *monoceros*), that made them more dangerous when males would battle for dominance.

The Middle Eastern variation of the unicorn, called a *Karkadan*, was a wild and powerful beast. This version has perhaps the most interesting natural history. Scientists and historians have speculated that the Karkadan was a misidentified rhinoceros, but this theory has been mostly disproven. The Karkadan featured most prominently in world history when, in the only known instance of domestication, Alexander the Great rode one in battle. His military exploits are legend and were only enhanced by riding a fierce creature capable of impaling its adversaries. He would go on to ride his Karkadan (named Bucephalus) for nearly a decade and conquer most of the known world.

The Karkadan would appear numerous times in world history and feature prominently in the Hebrew Bible. The creatures were written about extensively by scholars from Pliny the Elder to Ctesias to Leonardo da Vinci. It should be stressed that unicorns were not written about as mythological creatures during these times but as known entities. They did maintain certain spectacular qualities however. For instance, drinking from a vessel made from their horn provided magical healing properties, and, weirder still, unicorns were drawn to virgins. In fact, the best way to catch them was to lure them with a maiden and capture them while they slept in her lap.

That night at dinner at the hotel in Kinlochleven I was really in my element. We had spent the day hiking through the Scottish countryside joking with our new friends about politics and mythical creatures. Now we were sitting down to dinner after sampling a few fine Scottish whiskeys. Irwin continued to joke about unicorns and how they summed up the Scottish people: fearless and impossible to tame. I slept soundly that night and looked forward to starting our hiking early the next morning so that we could make it to Fort William with a side trip to the top of Ben Nevis.

Halfway to Fort William on the following day, the last day of our hike, our journey took a turn. Not far off the trail, we spotted a pasture with a small herd of Highland cattle. These are the coolest looking cows on the planet. They are an ancient breed of cattle with long horns, a thick and shaggy coat which is typically red, and an enormous mop of hair on their heads. The Highland cattle I met on my previous trip to Scotland were all friendly (not all breeds of cow are friendly), so I cautiously walked up to the fence and my friends followed. We were vets after all, and these creatures were fascinating. They almost don't look real. As we talked to the cows trying to draw them closer, the farmer stepped out from a stone outbuilding only about a hundred yards away.

At first I expected him to tell us to move along and stop bothering his cows, but he was a chatty type and soon learned that we were a group of veterinarians out for a walk on the Way. Jan appeared to be his favorite, and soon he was asking her a variety of questions about her career as a large animal vet in New York. As the conversation was wrapping up, she wanted to make clear to the farmer (Herb was his name) that it was a pleasure meeting him by chance like this and that these were the strangest and most attractive hoof stock she had ever seen in all her years. "I've got one stranger," was his reply. Really? What kind of cow? It wasn't a cow actually. We then played a game of what resembled twenty questions. Was it bigger than these cows? No. Was it domesticated? No. Could we see it? Maybe. Was it healthy? Not likely.

The guy definitely knew how to get our attention. We were fascinated with his replies. After continued questioning, we learned that he had taken in a sick, wild animal he'd found in the neighboring countryside and had been trying to nurse it back to health so that he could release it. I was having some serious *déjà vu* as the situation developed. At some point during our chat along his property line, I suspected that it dawned on farmer Herb that this chance meeting with a walking party of veterinarians may be just the help he needed. Eventually he asked us, with a wry smile on his face, "Can you keep a secret?" We all perked up a little more and answered in the affirmative. This guy wanted us to check out his mystery animal.

He led us across the pasture into his main barn. The building was modest but contained a number of stables, a tack room, a dining/kitchen/food prep area and, off at one end, a separate set of stables. As we approached the more private stables, he muttered: "You are not going to believe this. Still can't believe it myself." The stable containing the patient had a large blanket hanging in front of the stall. I presumed this was done for privacy. We often hang a towel on the kennel door of nervous cats to give them a little privacy.

Herb escorted Jan up to the stall and slowly pulled aside the blanket so that she could see the contents. She poked her head into the gap and stared for a good while. She turned, smiled at me, and said, "Dr. Otterson needs to see this. It's his specialty." The anticipation was killing me as I approached the stall. I really don't handle stress well. To be more exact, I don't handle anticipation well. As

I stated before, waiting, worrying and anticipating make me crazy. Before a major surgery or an appointment where a cat may be really sick, my anxiety (inherited from my mother's side) makes me unnaturally nervous. Once I start in on the procedure or the exam, I am fine. As I looked at the patient in Herb's secret stall, I became deliriously happy. Herb had found an injured unicorn while off traveling in the Highland near Ben Nevis!

His description of the rescue sounds almost like my father finding the jackalope in the Arizona desert. He was out with a friend a couple days ago when they came upon what they thought was an injured deer laying off in the tall grass. It was sitting sternally with its head down, and, as they approached, it weakly lifted its head, trying to stand and get away. Then it collapsed.

They did not notice the single horn at first. What they saw was a hundred-pound brown ungulate too weak to stand. Their first thought was that it had been hurt, either from a collision with a car or a hunter's shot that had not been fatal. They approached with caution. An injured animal can be really dangerous. Being experienced farm hands, their first concern before inspecting the creature was to control the head. Herb cautiously approached the head but could find only one long central twisted horn to grasp. He grabbed the horn and started to look at the head. His friend, Peaches, slid up next to him and started examining the rest of the "deer". No bullet wounds, bleeding or broken legs. They needed to get this beast out of the elements and give it some TLC.

It was as they lifted and maneuvered "the deer" into the back of Herb's van that they realized that it was not actually a deer but perhaps a unicorn. Herb closed the rear door and slid in next to the creature to try to provide restraint and calming for the drive back to his farm. It would take about thirty minutes of driving. During the trip, they tried to sort out what was happening. Herb's recounting of the drive sounded oddly familiar to me and contained an assortment of the following phrases. "What the hell is it?" "It's a unicorn." "That's impossible." "What are we going to do?" "They don't exist." "Apparently they do." "It's our national animal. Isn't it?" "I think it's an antelope with a deformed horn." "We have to save it. It's the Scottish thing to do." "We're going to be famous." "We're going to be locked up in the looney bin." "What makes a unicorn sick? I thought they were supposed to cure all that ails you."

Once at the barn, they backed the vehicle almost all the way to the stall and were able to gently move him on in. They offered him water and he drank. Herb then thought to call his regular vet. He'd known the guy for ages and trusted him. Then it dawned on him that his vet was on vacation out of the country. Dare they call someone else? They decided to watch the unicorn and think it over. They each had a ton of experience with farm animals and hoped that they could figure out how to make him feel better. They returned to the principle that I had mentioned many pages ago—treat the exotic creature before you as you would the nearest domestic that you know, and use common sense.

The unicorn before them weighed about 100 pounds, had cloven hooves and looked a lot like a cow or, more correctly, a deer. They had inspected him and he seemed otherwise young and healthy. They did not see any signs of trauma, but he was clearly weak. They correctly presumed that a healthy unicorn would not let a couple guys carry him into a vehicle for transport without a fight. Scottish folklore describes them as ferocious. One of the ways to capture them advises you to stand before a tree and have them charge you. At the last moment, you step out of the way and the horn becomes stuck in the tree. This guy was not charging anyone. He was weak and obviously in some kind of distress.

Peaches suggested hardware disease (or, in medical Latin-speak, traumatic *reticuloperitonitis*) as the cause of his malaise. (He'd named him *Not Your Little Pony* by this point.) Cows are notorious for swallowing just about anything left in a field or accidentally put in their feed—nails, screws, barbed wire, wedding rings, car keys—a cow will eat it. Once ingested, the metal will knock around in the cow's stomach irritating the mucosa, occasionally poking through the stomach wall and potentially leading to an infection that might actually be fatal. Hardware disease is so common that feed stores (and just about any large animal supply store) actually sell cow magnets. You give the magnets orally to year-old cows and they pass into their famous four-chambered stomach and wait. When the cow eats something stupid, the magnet sticks to the object and prevents it from cutting into the stomach wall.

What if Not Your Little Pony had eaten some strange metal object that was making him sick? What harm was there in giving him a cow magnet and seeing if it made him feel better? They had an extra magnet sitting around so they got him to swallow it and then they gave him more water. Over the next day or so, he seemed a little better. He drank water, ate a little hay, and stood up a couple times, but he was still not quite right. They concluded that he needed a vet, and that was the morning we walked up to the field. While we sat staring at the unicorn, Herb sent for Peaches to bring Herb's ten-year-old son Eric to the barn. Herb noted to us that the unicorn was calmer when his son was present. I pointed out that folklore was full of tales of unicorns attracted to or calmed by virgins. The use of virgins in the capture of unicorns is actually described by Leonardo da Vinci in his writings. Da Vinci had a bit of a unicorn obsession as he made numerous sketches and paintings with them, usually with a maiden. As with most farm kids, Eric had been essentially raised in a barn and would likely be helpful to have around.

As we sat outside the stall and discussed our options, it became clear that we needed a diagnosis. It's the foundation of medical training to try and make a definitive diagnosis before initiating treatment. For that, we needed an x-ray of this unicorn's abdomen, and we needed it quick. If an x-ray showed suspicious metal objects in his stomach, we would then have to perform the world's first unicorn rumenotomy in order to get the metal out. Irwin called his classmate Gordon who was an equine practitioner near Fort William. Surely he had a portable radiograph machine and would be able to clarify whether there was metal in the unicorn's stomach. We had changed his name to *Our Little Pony* by now. Gordon was out on field calls but would be able to meet us at the barn within about an hour.

Horse vets use portable x-rays a lot, mainly to look at injured legs. These x-ray units are not very powerful but they should be able to assess this modest abdomen. Fortunately Gordon had recently purchased a new digital machine which meant that we would get nearly instant results. I should note at this point that Gordon was a delightful fellow and strangely unfazed to be taking an x-ray of what appeared to be a unicorn. With Eric petting the unicorn and speaking softly in his ear, Gordon positioned the machine and x-ray plate and calmly snapped an image. We walked with Gordon as he took the x-ray plate out to his truck to load the data onto his laptop.

The interpretation of x-rays is both an art and a science. At its heart, it is a logic puzzle in creative anatomy and pathology. You take a two-dimensional image of your patient in white, black and a lot of gray in between and try to sort out the problem. Today, a child could have diagnosed it. In fact, a child did diagnose it. We all sighed as the image materialized on the screen while Eric blurted out, "Why is there a chain in his belly?" Our friend had swallowed about twenty links of a metal chain, and it appeared to be caught up in the chambers of his stomach. No wonder he felt so lousy.

This chain needed to come out. It had to be irritating the mucosa of the stomach, would eventually cause an obstruction, and could even be causing heavy metal poisoning. We put our heads together to figure out what was best for Our Little Pony. My first suggestion was a rumenotomy. It sounds like science fiction, but large animal vets commonly use lidocaine to numb the flank of cows and then perform abdominal surgery on an awake and standing patient. I watched it once in vet school, and it blew my mind. Jan and Irwin's reaction was one of shock. I wanted them to do what? And on a unicorn? It was at this point that Gordon suggested that we simply pull the chain out using his practice partner's new endoscope. That would be so much easier on the patient and would not require an actual surgery, hence a faster recovery and a more favorable return to the wild. It made total sense.

His colleague had purchased the endoscope second-hand a few months ago. Endoscopes are common practice in human medicine today, and veterinarians have been using them for decades. We use them for the same procedures that our MD colleagues do, but vets often use them to remove foreign objects from dog stomachs. Just last week, Gordon's partner removed a sock from the stomach of one dog and a rubber ducky from another. You are likely asking yourself, why would a unicorn swallow a chain? Upon seeing the chain on the x-ray, I immediately reflected on the famous tapestry *The Unicorn Is Penned* from the 15th century. I'd seen this work of art in person at the Metropolitan Museum of Art in Manhattan when I was visiting my brother as a teenager. In the tapestry, a white unicorn is in a circular wooden pen and is chained by a collar to a tree. As I played detective, it seemed to me that some idiot had probably used a maiden to capture Our Little Pony and tried to contain him with a chain. In the act of breaking free, he must have eaten the remains of his chain and made himself sick.

The actual procedure to remove the chain was a little anti-climactic given the profound anticipation we felt leading up to it. Irwin and Jan, under the supervision of our board-certified anesthesiologist Edgar, gave him a combination of sedatives that Gordon had in his truck. OLP became woozy in about a minute and Edgar and Rebecca sat on each side to stabilize him. As he started to relax, it was my first real opportunity to take a good look at our patient. It was both amazing and a bummer. This unicorn was the most beautiful antelope I had ever seen. I guessed that he weighed about 120 pounds with a muscular build and a thick, light brown mottled coat. The horn was about 18 inches long, off white, and twisted with a taper to a blunt tip. It could clearly do some damage.

How many of these creatures existed in the wilds of Scotland was anyone's guess. Scotland was full of remote and rugged places, and why this one ventured close enough to civilization was un-certain. You could see how his markings would blend in with the surroundings. He was small in stature, allowing him to be silhou-etted with the moor grasses. The last known sighting in Europe was in the sixteenth century. His Middle Eastern and Asian rela-tives had lived in more populated parts of the world and had been thought to be extinct for centuries. As I looked at the horn, I reflected on the time in vet school that I had assisted in the anesthesia of a captive eland (a several hundred pound African hoofstock) at a research and breeding facility for endangered species outside New Orleans. During the recovery, the creature flailed back into a stall wall nearly impaling my instructor with its horns. As I quickly relived that moment, I cautioned my colleagues that, while this appeared to be going well, we were entering new territory.

The endoscope was passed with ease down the esophagus and into the first chamber of the stomach. I could watch on the screen as Gordon approached the chain with the open jaws of the endoscope. After a couple failed attempts, he grasped on to the end link and began to pull the entire scope out from OLP. He met a little resistance on the way, but with a little wiggling, out came about two feet of chain with what appeared to be a large dog collar at the end.

Sometimes being a vet feels like being a detective. What series of events led to a unicorn swallowing a section of chain with a collar attached? Best we could figure, someone had captured this lovely creature and, unsuccessfully, tried to restrain him with a collar. Countless tales from mythology relate that confining a unicorn is a pointless endeavor. This unicorn had broken free and for some reason had eaten his chain and collar. I'm not sure exactly how smart unicorns are, but I guess I can appreciate the symbolic eating of the chain that once bound you.

As I explained in the first three chapters, an animal rehab is not fully successful until the patient is released into the wild and able to survive on its own. While Jan, Irwin, and Gordon were conducting the medical part of this procedure, Herb and I started making plans for Our Little Pony's rapid transit back to the wild. We decided that we would recover the unicorn from anesthesia in the back of Herb's van while we sped back to the site where he had initially been found (or to the nearest wild spot that our limited time allowed). I offered to ride in the back and attempt to restrain the unicorn while he woke up and Herb suggested his son Eric ride along as the unicorn seemed to like him best.

As soon as the chain and collar were removed, Gordon and Jan reinserted the endoscope to look throughout the stomachs for additional foreign material or damage to the mucosa. After a minute or so, they were satisfied that the stomachs were empty and relatively healthy. We immediately transferred the still-sedated Our Little Pony to the back of the van and I jumped in beside him carrying a bunch of blankets. Jan hopped in next to me despite my protests that there was limited room. "You're out of your league, Cat Boy," she said with a huge smile.

She was right. Waking up a horse from anesthesia was one of the scariest events I had experienced as a vet student. (The scariest was when a fatigued reptile handler accidentally dropped an adolescent rattlesnake on my boots.) Sometimes large animals wake up smoothly from a procedure, but sometimes, given that they are prey animals, they wake up running and freaking out.

Herb left his farm like he was qualifying for NASCAR. His son was in the front seat looking back and singing nursery rhymes to his unicorn. It had a calming effect on all of us. Jan and I sat on both sides of the patient staring across the valley at Ben Nevis and the sur-

European Unicorn
Monoceros europa

rounding mountains. We had just exited on to some dirt roads and the road had gotten rougher. More importantly, we were leaving civilization. I looked across the unicorn horn and asked Jan: "Aren't you glad you invited me to the conference?" Her smile and head shaking said it all. Jan had recovered countless animals in decades as a country vet. I had already agreed to do what she said and stay away from the horn.

Fortunately this unicorn was not that large, about the size of a small deer. We laid a thick blanket over him and, after fifteen minutes of driving, he was starting to move around pretty strongly. We had reached an expanse of moor with some rather tall grasses. It was time to stop and let him go. Jan noted that the tall grass would provide some camouflage and the soft earth would provide some cushion when he fell.

We lifted him, blankets and all, and carried him twenty yards from the car. Herb pulled away as we did not want him charging the car after mistaking it for a lion. When we couldn't control his struggling anymore, we lifted the blanket and watched him stumble to his feet. He reminded me of the newborn hoofstock I had watched on nature videos trying to figure out how their spindly legs worked. I imagined that he had to be relieved to be out in the open spaces again. Then the most remarkable thing happened: He walked unsteadily for about fifty yards and laid down in a patch of thick grass. Newborn deer do this. They shelter in tall grass for the first few days of their lives and wait for their mothers to come nurse them. They cozy into the grass and essentially disappear.

Sundown had occurred about 30 minutes earlier and it was getting dark. The timing could not have been better for the unicorn. All he had to do was rest there and sleep off his anesthesia hangover. The second vehicle had caught up with us by now and we all waited and watched from a distance—no night vision goggles this time. In the morning, he was gone. He'd likely woken up before sunrise and walked off into the Highlands.

We returned to Herb's house, and he made us breakfast. Not a Scottish breakfast (with stewed tomatoes, blood pudding and stinky fish), but a normal breakfast of coffee and crumpets (the real English muffin) and jam. Herb was exhilarated. We'd saved his unicorn! My walking party proceeded to tell him about my experiences with the chupacabra, sasquatch, plesiosaur, and the fairies. Finally, people were starting to believe me. If I could only spend the rest of my life traveling the world enlisting people in the rescue of these creatures, I could have some credibility.

On the following day, Jan, Rebecca, and I flew home from Glasgow. By chance, we departed the airport on a northeast heading which meant that we had fantastic views of Brannoch Moor and Ben Nevis. Our eyes scanned the landscape searching in vain for Our Little Pony. Off in the distance, you could see Loch Ness as it is a remarkably long and large lake. The flight would become a bird's eye tour of my cryptid experiences. After several hours of flying over the Atlantic Ocean, we approached North America with Newfoundland featured prominently out the starboard window. Our flight would culminate with a descent over the Ontario woods and into Pearson Airport near Toronto. I spent most of the flight staring out at the planet below with thoughts of sasquatch, mermaids, and unicorns.

It was on our jet lagged drive back to Buffalo that Rebecca initiated the conversation of what we had just experienced. We really had not discussed it much since the unicorn rescue. It was clear that the last few days had opened her eyes to the hidden world around her. It is human nature (at least for most of us) to accept the world around us as what has always existed. If you can't see it or hold it, it doesn't matter. This perception had definitely changed for all those touched by these magical creatures. But more importantly, they had been shown that the natural world they had known was equally wondrous.

Most people are unaware that the Audubon Society was founded in response to the Great Plume War. Nineteenth century fashion required that cultured ladies adorn themselves, and in particular their hats, with exotic feathers. The more lovely the feather, the more valuable the bird, and the more threatened the bird population became. As awareness of the ecological nightmare the pursuit of feathers was causing, both the Audubon Society and the Nature Conservancy were created to preserve habitat and change attitudes about reckless destruction of nature. One of the Audubon Society's mottos remains "Protect birds and we protect the Earth."

As we were crossing the Canadian border into Buffalo, we found ourselves debating the merits of going public with our experiences. Could we share our new appreciation of the world? Would Caribbean nations be more likely to preserve habitat knowing that the survival of the chupacabra relied on their efforts? Both the endangered Atlantic Right Whale and merfolk would benefit from more sensible shipping and fishing practices. And the production of fossil fuels was harming all creatures. Progress has been made in reducing the poaching of endangered species like elephants and rhinos, but to what lengths would a criminal go to bag a sasquatch, or a unicorn and its magical horn? Humans are unique in the animal kingdom in having the awareness to understand self-determination. Could knowing that the species described in these pages actually exist be enough to tip our own species on to a more thoughtful and less destructive path? Does knowing that mermaids and unicorns really do exist make our world precious enough to preserve it?

I hope so.

EPILOGUE

I FEEL OBLIGATED TO MAKE A less-than-subtle plea for we humans to seek a more compassionate relationship with our surrounding world. It has become painfully clear that we are overpopulating the planet and destroying the natural world. There is an abundance of evidence that our reckless behavior toward the environment is affecting our own health and even resulting in the deaths of millions of people every year. On top of this, our actions and our negligence are devastating the creatures that share this planet, and are leading to an extinction rate comparable to the period that ended the reign of the dinosaurs 65 million years ago. This time we are the asteroid! We are in the middle of a human-caused extinction, and overlooked by most observers is the effect that our planetary destruction is having on cryptozoological creatures that live in the shadows and fringes of civilization. I don't think that British Petroleum really cared that the Deep Water Horizon disaster in the Gulf of Mexico resulted in the deaths of thousands of merfolk in addition to the fish and seabirds, but the rest of us should.

I am obligated to note that the publication of this book is in apparent violation of the confidentiality agreement I made with the UN when I entered the mermaid conservation program. Attorneys inform me, however, that this agreement has been null and void since the program was disbanded and reformed under another agency. In fact, the authorities deny that the program ever existed. I felt that the story of the Mer and their remarkable society deserved to be represented as part of this memoir.

BIBLIOGRAPHY

J.M. Barrie, *Peter Pan*, 1904

Jacques Cousteau, *The Silent World*, 1953

James Herriot, *All Creatures Great and Small*, 1972

Paul and Karin Johnsgard, *Dragons and Unicorns—A Natural History*, 1982

Elizabeth Kolbert, *The Sixth Extinction*, 2014

Farley Mowat, *Never Cry Wolf*, 1963

Farley Mowat, *Sea of Slaughter*, 1984

Barbara Rieti, *Strange Terrain—The Fairy World in Newfoundland*, 1991

Jules Verne, *Twenty Thousand Leagues Under the Sea*, 1870

ACKNOWLEDGEMENTS

I WOULD HAVE NEVER STARTED TO chronicle my experiences caring for cryptids without the support and encouragement of my wife, Laurie. As a reader, teacher, English PhD, she has been the perfect collaborator and her efforts to revise and improve what started out as a series of case studies in exotic veterinary medicine morphed into a memoir that gave me great pleasure to write. She is either sleeping or off on other adventures throughout these chronicles, but she is very much on every page. Our son, Nels, began participating in our family's adventures from the very beginning, and I am proud to have his contribution of the illustrations to capture the creatures we have seen.

Thanks to my parents Warren and Janet Otterson, my siblings Brad, Beth and Jill. Thanks to my dear Aunt Audrey for sharing so many stories about our family, and to her husband, Uncle Don, and his sons, DG and Mike, for taking me on adventures in the woods of Ontario. Thanks also for the encouragement from my niece Rebecca and her husband Henry.

Thanks to our favorite teacher Song Rio for guiding us through Puerto Rico and to my veterinary colleagues Drs. Pete Freyburger, Jim Albert, Jan Raines, Kevin Oppenheimer, Richie Burdeaux, Kevin Fitzgerald, and Michael Groves in proofreading and reviewing this manuscript and being great colleagues.

Thanks to my Newfoundland friends and colleagues—Brad deYoung, Richard Greatbatch, Al Hay, Brian Sanderson, Ken Forward, Rod Campbell, Al Goulding, Conrad Foisy, and Rick Dittman. So many fond memories of that magical island.

Thanks also to my coworker Melissa Pond, LVT, for being a remarkable proofreader, and for my friend and linguist Ardis Eschenberg for her guidance.

Thanks also to Michael Mirolla at Guernica Editions for giving me the opportunity to put this work in print and for my editor Gary Clairman. It's remarkable what professional editors can do for the ramblings of a lunatic.

Finally, I hope it's clear that these pages plead for everyone to value the world around us a little more. There is so much that is beautiful and magical and we need to care for it far better than we do.

ABOUT THE AUTHOR

TIMM OTTERSON (MS, DVM) WAS born in a US Army hospital on the island of Okinawa where his parents were stationed during the Vietnam War. He was raised on army bases in San Antonio and El Paso and later moved to Shreveport, Louisiana following his father's retirement from the service. He has a degree in Mechanical Engineering from Louisiana Tech University and a master's degree in ocean physics from Memorial University in St Johns, Newfoundland. He earned his veterinary doctorate at LSU in Baton Rouge and has resided for twenty years in Buffalo, New York where he practices at an all-feline clinic. He spends the remainder of his time enjoying outdoor activities and working in organized veterinary medicine, veterinary charities, and conservation work.